BeST
FRiends
for NeVer

Best Friends for Never

Adrienne Maria Vrettos

SCHOLASTIC PRESS | NEW YORK

All rights reserved. Published by Scholastic Press, an imprint of Scholastic Inc., *Publishers since 1920*. SCHOLASTIC, SCHOLASTIC PRESS, and associated logos are trademarks and/or registered trademarks of Scholastic Inc.

The publisher does not have any control over and does not assume any responsibility for author or third-party websites or their content.

Library of Congress Cataloging-in-Publication Data available

ISBN 978-0-545-56149-5

10 9 8 7 6 5 4 3 2 1   16 17 18 19 20

Printed in the U.S.A. 23

First edition, May 2016

Book design by Yaffa Jaskoll

for wren, for Desmond, and for Jeff

chapter one

In the shocked hush after it happens, I wonder if Zooey Dutchman Zervos had any idea when she sat down with her two yes-girls, Teagan and Tess, that she was about to get socially annihilated. Or maybe she thought she was just going to tear into some lunchtime cheese crackers while making side eyes at everyone in their general vicinity, per her usual. For some reason, the cheese crackers made the whole thing so much more awful to watch: She was eating them (with gusto!) when it happened. Just, like, totally chomping away, so when the bomb dropped and her mouth fell open in shock, you could see the mutilated nuclear orange sludge of chewed-up cheese crackers in her mouth.

I bet she's never able to eat cheese crackers again. I bet the sense memory will be too much for her and just the sound of the crinkly cellophane wrapper will lay her out flat and someone will have to get whatever the modern-day equivalent of smelling salts is. Rotten tuna fish? Poopy diapers? The smell of someone else's belly-button gunk? How *do* you revive someone whose heart is most likely a lump of coal?

"Oh my gosh." My best friend, Piper, stretches her small frame up to whisper in my ear. "That was *horrible!*"

I nod numbly in agreement as our friends Celeste and Fee, clueless about the noonday slaughter the rest of us sixth graders just witnessed, set down their lunch bags and slide onto the bench on the other side of our cafeteria table, completing our usual foursome.

Fee tips her head forward, so her thick curtain of black bangs edges over her big gray eyes. She lowers her voice to a theatrical purr and says to Piper, "Hiya, Pipes." Then nods at me and says in a tough-girl growl, "Brooklyn."

"Are you new here?" Celeste asks me, just like she has every day since she met me this summer. She asks with a grin that I can't help but return, despite the dire circumstances.

She slips off the thin barrette that keeps her springy brown curls from flopping over her face and prepares to slip it back in, but when I don't answer, she looks back and forth from me to Piper in confusion, still holding her clip. "What's going on?"

"Get OUT!" Fee practically yells, slamming her palm on the table and upsetting the handmade ALLERGY ALERT: THE ONLY NUT ALLOWED AT THIS TABLE IS PIPER sign we put out every day when we sit down. "Did I miss it?! Did something just go down between Zooey and the Ts?!"

Zooey and the Ts is what everyone calls Zooey and Teagan and Tess. They are, without question, the barbed point at the tippy-top of the sixth-grade popularity pyramid, gliding down the halls of Trepan's Grove Middle School in migrating-bird formation, with shiny, pop-star hair, their slender feet in ballet flats. They are what you expect popular sixth-grade girls in a wealthy small town to be like, at least if you've ever read a book or watched a PG-13 movie about middle school. They are the three kinds of pretty: pretty-looking, pretty rich, and pretty mean. I much prefer my friends' kind of pretty: pretty funny, pretty smart, and pretty-pretty when they laugh so hard they show all their teeth. Rae, my best friend in Brooklyn, was the same, except different.

Zooey and the Ts are what's known as Totally Popular, as opposed to me and my friends, who are more like Lower Medium Popular. Those are both actual classifications that people use here, according to Fee, who keeps track of things like that because she is *really* serious about Popularity and How to Attain It. She's so serious that she offers me information about popularity when I don't even ask for it and actually don't really want it because all of her information can be summed up in three words and one contraction: *We're not very popular.* Which is kind of a depressing thought even if you don't care about that sort of thing. Which I don't. Not really. I mean, I definitely didn't care about it when I went to a huge school in Brooklyn, and Rae and I were in our own happy little clique that consisted of the two of us and every single character in Tilde's Realm, which is otherwise known as the best fantasy series ever written. It is also unfortunately known as a Nerd Identifier. Fee taught me that, too, and thank goodness she did, because people in this picket-fenced apple town have a zero-tolerance policy for nerd behavior. Even if the rest of the world is starting to realize that nerds will inherit the earth (which, by the way, is printed on my favorite T-shirt, one that I will never wear again because that would expose my secret identity), I don't think Trepan's Grove ever got the memo. Their philosophy is more like Preppy=Popular, Nerds Need Not Apply. This worried Rae and me when we were doing online reconnaissance before I moved. "They're like . . . cyborgs," she said, leaning closer to the screen of her laptop to study a picture of a middle school picnic on the town website. "Everyone's so . . . sporty. And preppy. But not, like, ironically preppy. Just . . . preppy." She looked at me then, her face serious. "Don't let them change you, Hattie. Don't let them turn you into a cyborg." I assured her there was no way that would ever happen. Then I moved here. I wouldn't say I'm, like, one hundred percent cyborg at this point, but there are definitely some Hattie parts that have been replaced. It's the reason I don't text Rae goofy pictures of myself anymore. I'm kind of afraid of what she'll say when she sees that I actually have kind of changed.

"Tess and Teagan just, like . . ." I start to explain to Fee and Celeste, trying to find a way to put into words how their simple movement of abruptly standing up and leaving Zooey sitting alone in the middle of the cafeteria, her mouth full of orange cracker goo, was one of the most heartless things I'd ever seen. "They just, like, *abandoned* her."

Fee does a little gasp. "Really?" She cranes her neck to see Zooey stuffing her uneaten cheese crackers back into her lunch bag. "They just left her there? They didn't, like, say anything or anything?"

"She's like a polar bear adrift on a teeny-tiny chunk of ice," Piper says in disbelief.

"Yeah, an evil polar bear who pretty much deserves it," Fee adds.

Piper wrinkles her nose for a split second, making all of her freckles smoosh together into the shape of a stepped-on blueberry. "That was mean, Fee."

Fee huffs, still watching Zooey. "*I'm* mean? Zooey Dutchman Zervos made you cry every day of second grade, and *I'm* mean? Your mom still calls the school every summer to make sure you guys aren't in the same homeroom!"

"Fee!" Celeste scolds. "Stop staring!"

"I'm not staring," Fee says quickly, wrenching her gaze away from Zooey and dropping her excited look in favor of her usual studied, bored one. She gets her sandwich out of her bag and then glances back over to see which table Teagan and Tess have moved to. They're sitting with Jonah and Rico and a couple of other boys from the soccer team. Fee says Sitting with Boys at Lunch is a new development this year at Trepan's Grove Middle School, one that's only spread down as far as the Medium Popular kids. Piper and I agree this is a good thing, because who wants to see boys eat?

"I know Zooey's mean," Piper says quietly. "Especially with that new silent, evil glare thing she's doing this year, where she just, like, stares at you, letting you imagine the worst possible things about yourself." She shudders. "That's just some evil mind magic right there. Anyway, even with the evil mind tricks, she didn't deserve being dropped like that, in front of everyone."

Fee looks at us and says conspiratorially, "It just sucks it happened right before the Harvest Festival."

Ugh, I'd forgotten about the Harvest Festival!

"That *does* make it worse!" I whisper.

Fee nods at me in grave agreement.

Here is why even a newbie like me knows that the timing of what just happened is so awful: This entire town is one hundred percent bananas about two things: apples and the phrase "Remember that time at Harvest Festival . . ."

Piper has a whole wall in her attic bedroom covered top to bottom in photo-booth pictures and thumbtacked trinkets and other random stuff from every festival she's ever been to. There's a photograph of her second-grade class standing on a little outdoor stage on the town common, a teeny Piper in the front row, arms flung wide as she sings. "You'll be in these pictures this year," Piper told me, pointing to a messy row of photo-booth pictures, at least four of them starring Piper, Fee, and Celeste. My heart did a happy flip-flop when she said that, because goofy photo-booth pictures are a permanent record of a friendship. And even though I have a few things from the months since we became friends (Popsicle sticks from the snack shop at the town pond, movie ticket stubs), I desperately want something from the Harvest Festival.

Fee clucks her tongue. "Anyway, Zooey should have seen it coming."

"How could she have seen it coming?!" Piper objects, a little too loudly, scrambling up so she's sitting on the heels of her high-tops like a little kid, poking me in the side with a bony elbow in the process. "That was a total ambush!"

"Because," Fee says so quietly we have to lean in to hear her, "it was all over everywhere last night that Tess and Teagan were going to drop her."

"All over *where*?" Piper asks, exasperated, before glaring at the nut-free granola bar in her lunch, obviously debating if it was worth the little pieces that would get stuck in her braces.

"It was all over everything," Fee says knowingly. "On the *Internet*."

"Oh." Piper sighs so hard it's like she deflates. She passes the granola bar over to Celeste, who slides a ginger cookie across in return. "I was at my dad's last night and left my laptop at home. I couldn't do *anything* all night except kick his butt at Parcheesi."

"*You* saw, though, right?" Fee asks, looking at Celeste.

Celeste scoffs. "I was at the rink 'til late." She adjusts the zipper on the sleek black Ice Masters team sweatshirt, her name embroidered in crisp white cursive on the upper part of her right sleeve. Ice-skating is the reason I didn't meet Celeste until the very end of summer. She'd spent seven weeks studying with professional skaters at a rink in California. "And you know I don't participate in that kind of pollution of the spirit."

"Yeah, me either!" Piper says. "Celeste is right. That's spirit pollution, plain and simple." Sometimes I'm afraid that Piper is going to become best-best friends with Celeste instead of with me.

"Hattie?" Fee asks hopefully.

I shake my head. "I seriously doubt I have access to whatever site you're talking about." My mom and dad are super serious about keeping me from anything remotely resembling bullying or naked people online. *The Internet is full of turkeys. Remember that, Hattie,* my dad says. *And turkeys are stupid, stupid creatures.*

Fee huffs, "Your parents know you're not seven, right?"

Piper gives my arm a squeeze, the sort of thing she always does when the barbs poke out of Fee's tongue.

"Ugh! I can't even show you guys because it's all deleted already!" Fee says in frustration.

Piper's groan speaks for us all as we notice Zooey walking toward the exit—right by Tess and Teagan and the Boys Who Play Soccer at their table. The silence around Zooey grows with each step, until the only sound in the whole crowded cafeteria is the *pat pat pat* of her ballet flats on the linoleum. I wonder suddenly if she'll have to stop wearing ballet flats. If she has to turn them in at the Popularity Dismissal Counter, like when you hand in your bowling shoes to get your own shoes back. I wonder what they'd give her in return?

I mean, would I have to stop wearing high-tops with rainbow laces, corduroys that drive me crazy with their endless *zip zip zip* sounds, and my "stripy" if my friends suddenly dropped me? Would I go back to wearing T-shirts of cats doing funny things, and colorful leggings? Would I have to stop playing field hockey with Piper and Fee? Not that I would really *mind* having to stop playing field hockey. That sport is the worst.

As I watch Zooey, I think she's going to hurry by Teagan and Tess. If I were her, if that ever happened to me, I would run like the wind all the way back to Brooklyn. But Zooey comes to a stop right in front of them. ON PURPOSE. I gasp at her bravery and total lack of survival instinct.

"Oh my gosh," Piper whisper-squeaks, pulling the cuff of my sweatshirt so hard my hand falls off the table and onto her bent knees, where she grabs my fingers in a vise grip. "This is terrible! Make it stop!"

But I can't make it stop; none of us can. Celeste doesn't watch. She makes a point of taking out her hummus sandwich, but the rest of us can't look away.

Zooey is the first to speak, her strangled voice carrying across the hushed cafeteria. "Why?" she asks.

Her two as-of-four-minutes-ago best friends both raise their chins. The boys at the table look one hundred percent uncomfortable. A couple of them get up and move to another table. "Well," Tess says, with a glance at Teagan, like she's looking for approval, "you kind of turned into a total dork." Her voice breaks on the word *dork*, and she swallows so hard I can see her throat move.

"Why?" Zooey asks again.

Teagan snorts with impatience, rolls her eyes, and leans back in her chair before focusing her glare on Zooey.

Her voice doesn't crack at all. "Fine, if you want the details, *I'll* give them to you. You've become a total dork . . ."

"I said that already," Tess murmurs, looking put out.

Teagan gives Tess a sideways glare and continues. "You're a total dork, but *not* like adorkable, not like in a quirky way. You're just, like, *bizarre* in a bad way, you know . . . It makes people totally uncomfortable." Tess purses her lips and nods in serious, silent agreement. Teagan goes on, "And even though you *kind of* still wear the same clothes we do, they just look weird on you now for some reason, like your body is just, like"—she pauses, flicking her eyes up and down Zooey's frame, moving her hands as if to pat Zooey's shape—"*weirdly* built *wrong*, you know? Like you're, you know, *developing* in the wrong places or something."

Tess giggles a theatrical *"Oh my God!"* at this, and Teagan, acting like she's trying to stifle a laugh for Zooey's sake, says, "So that's it. You act weird, you look weird. Oh! And you smell weird. Like maybe you don't wash your—" We can't hear what she says because Tess lets out a delighted screamy laugh, but from the reaction of the people closer to the table, the rest of the sentence is pretty awful.

I exchange a horrified look with Celeste and Piper. Piper asks, "Should we do something?"

Celeste is already starting to get up. Piper is, too,

like maybe they're going to march over there and say something.

Fee quickly reaches across the table and grabs both of their wrists, keeping them still. She doesn't grab me but somehow holds me with a glare that's worthy of Zooey herself. "Don't move a muscle," she growls to all of us, her eyes bugging out in a not entirely appealing way. "You want them to turn on us next?"

I'm glad she says it, because that is *exactly* what I was thinking. Piper seems to consider this, but Celeste yanks her hand free from Fee's grip and steps over the bench, grabbing her lunch bag.

"It's too late," Fee says, with something like relief. I look over and see Ms. Eurki is walking quickly over to the battlefield. She says something quietly to Zooey, and Zooey leaves the cafeteria. Then Ms. Eurki says something even quieter to the Ts and they roll their eyes but put their lunch stuff away, get up, and follow Ms. Eurki out of the cafeteria.

Celeste sighs and gives Fee a look as she sits back down.

"What?" Fee asks indignantly. "I don't want them to ice us out. Is that so wrong?"

"Ice us out?" Celeste asks. "Ice us out of *what*?"

Fee gives an annoyed flip of her hair. "Forget it."

But Celeste won't forget about it. "And since when do you care about that sort of thing?"

I want to say *It's all she cares about!* But I hold my tongue as they stare each other down.

"Fiona," Celeste finally says.

"Celestia," Fee responds.

"I don't want to fight with you," Celeste tells Fee. "I love you more than peanut butter on crackers."

I poke Piper and whisper "*Ffftttt*," the sound of an EpiPen, which is what I always do when someone mentions a peanut product around us. She nods her thanks.

"And I love you more than popping bubble wrap," Fee responds.

"So can we stop fighting?"

Fee shrugs. "I'm not fighting. I'm just looking out for us."

chapter two

I pretty much have nothing in common with Zooey, apart from the fact that neither of us is a unicorn and we both live in Trepan's Grove. Other than that . . . I'm guessing she burst out fully formed from under a dew-covered leaf, wandered into school, and was immediately worshipped as a goddess. I bet no one knew she was evil until it was too late, until they had already called her queen and she wouldn't let them take it back. That's also basically the plot of Tilde's Realm #6: *Witchlure*, but I think it's probably an accurate summation.

But now there is at least one thing I *can* one hundred percent relate to Zooey on. It's the whole sitting-down-to-eat-without-knowing-your-life-is-going-to-change thing, because that's exactly how I ended up here in Trepan's Grove in the first place.

School had just ended for the year, and my mom and I were sitting and reading at the kitchen table, waiting for

Dad to get back with our breakfast bagels. In my memory, it was a perfect moment: the summer sun streaming through the window onto the table, warming both the morning paper and our gigantic gray cat, Champ, spread on top of it. There was a breeze, and the scent of jasmine from the backyard four floors below. I knew I would be spending some summer nights back there catching fireflies with the little kids who lived on the first floor until my mom would call out the kitchen window for me to come up and go to bed. It was going to be a *great* summer, even if Rae was going to be visiting family in the Dominican Republic for part of it.

"I was so happy in that moment!" I told Rae later. "I was just, like, *la-di-da*-ing my way through a Saturday morning, thinking about how you and me were going to meet up at the pool later, and then . . . BOOM. Dad came home, and he didn't just bring bagels. He brought a bomb."

Dad pulled the bagels, warm little bundles of happiness, from a white plastic bag printed with I ♥ NEW YORK. I'd put my book down on the table, using my index finger to save my page, and was trying to unwrap my bagel with the other hand, when I noticed that both my parents had gone still and were looking at me.

"What?" I asked, a little alarmed, my first thought being: *Bugs!* "Is there a bug?" I asked, staying perfectly still. "Is it on me? It's on me, isn't it? GET IT OFF!"

And that's when they dropped The Bomb: no bug, but something even worse. Dr. Liu, who was my dad's favorite dentistry professor, a guy he *still* quoted on major holidays—"Celebrate with sugar, pay the price with the drill"—was retiring. Again. He'd already retired from teaching at a college in the city years ago and had set up a practice in some podunk town in the middle of nowhere, something Dad had always joked about doing whenever the Yankees were winning or the subways broke down, two things that unfortunately happened all the time. Except now he wasn't joking. Dr. Liu was moving to Florida and selling my dad his practice. And Mom had found a nursing job at a local hospital. And we were leaving the apartment my parents had rented since before I was born. *Our* apartment. With its slanted floors and tyrannical radiators and sunny kitchen and a bathroom so small you could sit on the john and brush your teeth at the same time, unless your parents saw you and told you it was unhygienic. With the three sets of neighbors from three different continents who would sometimes bring up plates of food, depending on who was celebrating a holiday, and who would come to my dad with toothaches.

We were leaving Brooklyn, going to some random place called . . .

"Trepan's Grove?!" I wailed. "That's the name of a soap opera, not a town!"

"It's so cute! You'll love it!" Mom said, her voice going shrill with the effort of using exclamation points to convince me this would not be the worst thing that's ever happened in the history of our family, ever.

I looked out the window over the backyard. My school uniforms hung drying on the clothesline outside our window, freshly out of the wash and ready to be donated. I watched them sway a little in the breeze. "I don't *want* to move upstate!" I said, my chin quivering. Mom and Dad didn't say anything. "What?" I asked, a cold feeling of doom blooming in my belly.

"Well," Mom said carefully, "it's actually not upstate; it's in Massachusetts. Where Daddy's from."

"It's not even in NEW YORK?!" I screeched, jumping up and knocking over my chair. "Are you kidding me? Leave New York? Who does that?"

I could see that, for some reason, they found my outburst adorable, like when I disagree with them about what directions to give cabbies. "Don't smile at me, you traitors!" I shouted, righting my chair.

"Hattie, we just think that living in a place where you had more of a relation—"

My jaw dropped. "Oh my gosh, if you say 'RELATIONSHIP WITH NATURE,' I am going to scream and barf at the same time, and it's going to be DISGUSTING!"

"Hattie," my dad said, a warning in his voice.

I ignored him. "We have trees in New York. We have wildlife! We have squirrels and chipmunks and . . . and . . . and rats! We have whole colonies of rats just"—I wiggled my fingers—"skittering around the subways. That's nature!"

I couldn't keep my mouth from twisting into a smile as my parents fought back laughter.

"Oh, Hattie!" my mom said, pulling me into a hug. "I know it will be a big change, but you'll see. This is going to be wonderful for our family. We'll be close to your uncles and your cousins!"

They showed me some pictures then, on Dad's laptop, my first glimpse of Trepan's Grove.

"Cute, right?" my mom said, pointing out the town common with its green, sloping lawn. "That's the elementary school at the top. Look at the picket fence around the playground! And down there at the bottom." She clicked through another picture. "That's a statue of Joseph Trepan, the town's founder." I was beginning to think she'd rehearsed this little slide show. "You'll be going to the middle school. It's brand-new. Look at its library!" she trilled as I studied the images of a brick-and-glass building on top of a hill close to the adorable center of town. There were athletic fields hemmed in by gray stone walls.

"Built by Pilgrims!" Dad said. *I think!* My dad's new office didn't look like an office at all, because it was inside a pretty yellow Victorian house across from the town common. There was a neat brick path leading from the sidewalk up to the wide front porch, and at the foot of the path was one of those old-fashioned wooden signs that said DENTIST'S HOUSE, and below that hung a smaller sign reading DR. MATTHEW LIU. "Everybody in town says, 'I'm going to the Dentist's House,' when they have an appointment. Isn't that so small-town charming?" Mom said excitedly. Most of the houses around the common were like this, something out of a postcard, pretty old houses with gables and picket fences.

"So we get to live there?" I asked, pointing to the Dentist's House. "Upstairs or something?" The house was so cute, with its front porch and flower boxes, that maybe I was a *little* excited about living there.

"Oh, no," my mom said quickly, "we're renting a *great* place to live across town."

"Anyway!" Dad said, clicking to a picture of a small blue cottage with white trim and a glassed-in porch. "This is the Trading Post. It's like an old-fashioned general store. It's right on the common. They sell penny candy in little blue paper bags . . ."

I gasped and looked at Mom. *J'accuse!* I said, remembering the blue paper sack of candy she'd brought back when she and Dad went on a trip a few months ago, leaving me to sleep over at Rae's house.

"She's onto us!" Mom stage-whispered to dad. "I'm going to distract her with another hug."

"We're going to get eaten by bears," I said into her shoulder, as she squeezed me close.

"Not on our first day!" she said brightly.

Chapter Three

Mom was right. We haven't been eaten by bears.

But I came close!

I am sure that I was almost bear food on the Night That Would Not End, otherwise known as the night my new friends thought it would be fun to invite me camping in the woods behind Fee's farm to celebrate-slash-mourn the end of our first summer together.

Nobody told me that throwing a piece of apple pie as hard as I could into the woods when nobody was looking might attract bears. I would have just sucked it up and eaten the thing if I'd known that. I don't care if apple pie is the official town snack of Trepan's Grove, I think it's the most disgusting dessert ever created. But I didn't have the heart to tell my pie-loving friends that. Hence, the pie flinging. It wasn't until we were all tucked into our sleeping bags and Fee was zipping up the tent that I realized I'd basically flung a COME EAT US sign outside the tent. Fee had said, "You guys don't have any food, right?" Then she said in a funny voice, "Cuz this is BEAR COUNTRY!" and everyone laughed. Except me. Because even if I didn't have food in the tent, I knew there was some in close proximity because the truth is, I'm not super athletic, so throwing something as hard as I can means it's not going to go very far. And that's why, as soon as Fee had gotten into her sleeping bag, I announced I had to pee, and bravely said I was going to go in the woods because, you know, it's part of the experience, instead of walking the fifty yards back to Fee's farmhouse to use actual indoor plumbing.

Using a flashlight to search for apple pie in a dark forest is a terrifying experience. Actually, that part wasn't so bad. What was truly terrifying was that, once I saw the piece of smooshed pie on the ground, I was suddenly gripped with a frantic urgency and grabbed the slimy mess, clutched it to my heart, and then ran as fast and as far as I possibly could into the dark forest, my pulse thumping in my ears, my flashlight beam bouncing and shaking on the ground in front of me, until I could go no farther, and I heroically flung the piece of pie away from me into the darkness, into the inky maw of the forest. As my breath slowed and the sweat cooled on my skin, I raised a victory fist in the air. And then I turned to follow the lights of Fee's farmhouse back toward the tent but discovered the lights were gone.

Here's what I was taught to do if I ever got separated from my parents in Brooklyn. If I got off the subway and they didn't, then I was to stand on the platform and wait for them to get off at the next stop, get on another train, and come back for me. Same thing goes with elevators. If we got separated in a crowd, I was to stay in one place for a few minutes, and then if they didn't come back, find some lady with kids and ask to use her phone. Though the few times it happened to me, someone always noticed the panicked look on my face before I even had a chance to ask for help, and then stood there with me until Mom or Dad pushed through the crowd with panicked looks of their own.

But Mom and Dad never went over What to Do When Lost in a Deep Dark Forest Full of Bears.

I took a step and then thought maybe I should stay in one place, and then I took a step back to exactly where I'd been. And then . . . I'm not going to say that nature and I "had a moment." It's not that standing there in the cool summer darkness, I fell in love with the great outdoors and all it has to offer and now I'm going to be outside all the time on purpose . . . It's just that, all of a sudden, I understood two things: darkness and silence—and that there really was no such thing as either one in the forest. You just have to stand still for a minute and you'll hear and see all sorts of things.

The best thing I saw were pinpricks of light sweeping back and forth, flickering between the tree trunks, and the faint sounds of my friends' voices. *"Hattie! Hattie!"*

I screamed out, louder than I ever had before, my voice powered by fear and relief and self-preservation, "I'M HERE!"

Which is when I was suddenly engulfed in a beam of light from the back porch of Fee's next-door neighbors, in whose wooded yard it turned out I was standing and onto whose back porch I had flung my piece of pie. The neighbor lady stepped in it with her bare feet when she came out to investigate why there was a screaming kid in her backyard, and I think she thought it was dog poop because as she stepped in it, she yelled out, "UGH!" and then sort of shook her foot at the same time that she was saying, "Are you okay?" And then she yelled, "AAAHHHH!" because all of my friends came tearing out of the forest at that very moment, screaming their heads off and tackling me with hugs so hard we fell into her kids' sandbox, a tangle of pajama pants and headgear. I ended up with a sleeping bag over my face ("We brought it because what if we found you and you were hypothermic?"), half a bottle of Gatorade down my front ("Because you might have been dehydrated!"), and Celeste's knee on top of my right ankle, making it bend in a new and painful way. I didn't have the heart to tell her she'd kneecapped my ankle, so I kind of pretended I'd twisted it in the woods.

The Goodys' neighbor grumbled and washed off her pie-coated foot with the garden hose as my friends sat on the wooden rim of the sandbox and watched, with the giddy giggles that come post-adrenaline-rush, as Mr. Goody tenderly felt around my ankle and declared it probably sprained but not broken. With a stern look, he silenced my friends' request to let them carry me using the three-person stretcher technique they'd learned in Girl Scouts, and instead carefully picked me up himself and accepted the neighbor's offer of a lift back to the farm.

It was that night, gathered at the Goodys' farmhouse table, cracking up as we relived our adventure, that something in our new friendship slid into place. My ankle was propped on the chair next to me, resting on an apple-shaped pillow and covered with a growing mound of the frozen vegetable packages that Piper kept disappearing to fetch from the freezer, returning each time to place them carefully upon my ankle, and laughing so hard, tears streamed down her cheeks. We took turns reenacting my desperate cry in the woods—"I'M HERE!"—and I laughed tearfully as my friends explained just how scared they were when I didn't come back from peeing in the woods.

The Goodys had me call my parents and tell them

what had happened, and then Mom and Dad talked to Mrs. Goody, who assured them I was okay and welcome to stay. By that time, it was past three in the morning, and we were all one hundred percent awake. So Mr. Goody made us middle-of-the-night pancakes and bacon and hot chocolate. But before I had any of that, my friends, who had disappeared from the table, solemnly reentered the room. Piper was in the lead, holding a plate high in front of her, and it took me a moment to realize that a lit birthday candle was on top.

"In honor of the fact that you were not eaten by a bear and that you didn't fall off a cliff into the gully—"

"I didn't even know that was a possibility!" I yelped.

Piper giggled, then continued. "Or get stung to death by hornets or trapped between a rock and a hard place or—"

Fee snorted, "Come on, Pipes."

Piper set the plate in front of me. "We present you with this We're Glad You're Alive, Hattie, Pie. Please eat!"

"Oh, um . . ." I faltered, looking at the plate-size slice of apple pie, a pink glob of candle wax pooling in its center. "I love it!"

chapter
four

It took the whole last week of summer vacation for my ankle to heal, a week of my dad calling me Igor and my mom checking the swelling each morning before driving me to the town pond, where I would spend the day on Piper's giant blanket under a willow tree, playing hearts with my friends. Most evenings that week, I would come home and find a delivery of back-to-school clothes waiting, and I'd sit on the couch with my sore ankle on the coffee table and work my fingers into the thick plastic shipping bags and tear them open, excited and a little nervous to see what was inside.

Fee was actually the one who ordered most of the stuff for me the week before I hurt my ankle, clicking skillfully through site after site, adding things to shopping bags like she was checking them off a list, occasionally asking my size or color preference but mostly just joking that she was my personal shopper and knew what was best. I stood hovering behind where she sat at my desk in my bedroom, sometimes switching to perch nervously on the edge of my bed where Piper and Celeste sat with their heads pressed together, flipping through my old elementary school memory books, before I would jump up to look over Fee's shoulder again.

"Pipes," Fee said at one point, "you should let me pick out some new stuff for you!"

Piper snorted in response. "Please. My mom still has eleven industrial-size trash bags full of my sisters' hand-me-downs in the attic for me to get through, and, like, three-quarters of that are the exact same things you're looking at, except just different enough to make me look like a total dork. I'm lucky she buys me new underwear."

Fee harrumphed. "Celeste?" Celeste turned a page in my third-grade memory book before she answered. "I'm good. I'll be wearing mainly skate stuff anyway. Easier than changing after practice before school. Why do we have to be matchy-matchy anyway? We're not Zooey and the Ts."

Fee didn't respond, just clicked extra hard through to another website. I couldn't actually buy anything right that second. I needed Mom for that. So that night, she and I went through all of the stuff Fee had put into the shopping bags, deleting bunches of it until what I chose was within the budget Mom gave me, plus my leftover birthday money. This led to a neat stack of new clothes that I arranged and rearranged each night in the days before school started. I had corduroys I was determined to like despite the fact that they were sure to make that annoying *zip zip zip* sound, and a certain type of jeans and these shirts I'd never heard of and Converse high-tops, which I actually really liked. Most important, I had a "stripy," which was a brightly striped zip-up sweatshirt with a hood, lined with thick faux sheep fur. It's the most expensive thing we bought, and Mom said, "Better hope your arms don't grow, because I am never spending that much on a sweatshirt again." That's the item I tried on the most. I didn't expect Celeste to ditch hers for her skating sweatshirt.

By the time the first day of school came, the tenderness in my ankle was gone, and my attention shifted to a different kind of discomfort: the feeling you get in your belly the moment before you leap from a great height, like your stomach makes the jump before you do. Because what if certain clothes and six weeks of summer weren't enough to carry a friendship over into the school year? Actually, it was six weeks with Piper and Fee. Celeste had come home in mid-August, so when school started, I'd only known her a couple of weeks. That's like no time at all in a town where people remember each other in diapers.

It turns out there was no reason to worry. I *zip-zip-zipped* through the glass double doors of school the first day, and before I even had a chance to stand awkwardly in the fancy front atrium, figuring out where to go, Piper was beside me, grinning her toothy Piper grin, linking her arm through mine, and pulling me toward the sixth-grade locker corridor, where Celeste and Fee were waiting with a piece of apple pie. "It's your Happy First Day of School, Hattie, Pie!" Piper said gleefully.

"Oh! Wow!" I said, the butterflies in my stomach replaced by wiggling slimy worms. "Thanks!"

It wasn't until lunch on that first day, when I finally had the chance to eat something that would take away the awful taste of apple pie, that I started to wish my ankle had taken just a little longer to heal. Because that's when Coach Thackary and the other coaches got up in front of the salad bar and announced when tryouts would be for the fall sports teams. Kids actually cheered. Like foot-stomping, table-slapping *cheers*. For *sports*. It was one of the weirdest things I'd ever seen. The enthusiasm! It would have been contagious if enthusiasm for sports was something I was interested in catching.

I mean, not everybody cheered. Zooey and the Ts, for three. Zooey just glared while the Ts snickered and said things to each other. Piper told me that the Ts were on the soccer team but Zooey *just doesn't do sweat*.

"Are you *stoked*?!" Fee asked us, her smile all dimply, until she looked at Celeste.

"Celestia?" she asked, in this funny, coaxing way. "Why are you not cheering for Coach Thacka-Wacka?"

Celeste swallowed. "Because I'm not going out for field hockey."

"WHAA?" Fee said, and even though she said it in her funny voice, I exchanged a look with Piper. We could both tell Fee was upset.

"Don't make me feel bad about it," Celeste said quickly. "Mom said I had to choose between field hockey and skating. I can't do both. I mean, I could, but I wouldn't be able to give my all to either one, so what would the point be? I had to choose, and I chose skating."

Fee pressed her lips together, then said, "But field hockey is our thing."

"You could start skating again," Celeste said. "You were really good."

"Forget it," Fee said shortly. "I understand. I'm sad. Like, devastated. But I guess I get it."

"It will be fine," Celeste said, her voice turning hard. "Hattie will play field hockey, right, Hattie? You'll replace me." Her voice was so un-Celeste-like that I was too shocked to do anything but nod in agreement.

Here's how you get on the field hockey team: At tryouts, run as fast as you can in the opposite direction of the ball, and then wait in a state of complete panic as it gets whacked closer and closer to you. Then take your club and hit it as hard as you can to get it away from you before you are attacked by a mob of club-wielding athletes.

Of course, they call them field hockey sticks, not clubs, but you can't fool me. Those things are weapons.

Coach Thacka-Wacka said I showed good defensive instincts and laughed when I told her I was just trying really hard not to get killed. Then she put me on the team, and I've been running for my life three practices and a game a week ever since.

But today, being Harvest Festival Eve: There is NO field hockey practice! In fact, they canceled *all* after-school activities. I guess the thinking is that everyone else needed to conserve their energy because of the Harvest Festival, which should tell you something about how serious they are about the festival. Because the only thing they like more than apples here are sports.

The weather started to cool just a few weeks after school started and now, in mid-October, I am thankful to have my stripy to pull out of my locker when the last bell rings. I join the stream of kids pushing out through the glass front doors of school and smile when I breathe in the chilly air. Newly fallen leaves make a colorful carpet on the ground. I know, by winter, they will turn brown and crunchy and depressing. But for now, they're lush and bright.

"HATTIE!" my friends call out to me in goofy, dramatic unison as I step outside. They're already sitting on one of the cozy wooden benches that line the circular courtyard in front of school.

"I'M HERE!" I call back, and then I theatrically limp toward them through the crowded courtyard, my right Converse sneaker bumping over the cobblestones as I drag my foot.

"FESTI-VAL! FESTI-VAL!" Piper calls out to me, pumping her arms in victory. "Hattie's first festi-val!"

I hear a few people shout out what sounds like either *JINX* or *JANX* in response to Piper's cheer, which I make a mental note to ask Piper about later. I've realized that people say all sorts of whackadoo stuff in this town, inside jokes from preschool, and Piper is my dictionary app to figure things out.

Like the reason that whenever Siobhan Greene stands up to read a report or give a presentation, everyone mutters "*Bonjour*" is because she studied at a fancy French preschool and insisted on doing all of her homework in French for all of first grade.

I reach my friends and flop down across all three of their laps, a comfy bed of coordinating corduroys. "Holy cannoli," I say with a happy sigh, pulling the sleeves of my stripy sweatshirt over my chilly hands. "I really missed you guys!" Celeste and Fee have their heads tipped together, a set of shared earbuds supplying the silent-to-everyone-but-them sound track that makes them both croon, "Give me a chaaaaance," spreading their arms wide and then collapsing into giggles.

Piper grins down at me, the swoop of her blond surfer bangs hanging over one eye, her braces glinting in the sun. She pulls one of my tiny curls and gives a Ramona Quimby–worthy *boing!* "You saw us, like, literally, three minutes ago in bio lab."

"I know!" I exclaim. "And it was the longest three minutes of my *life*!" I sit up, wiggling to make room for myself on the bench, taking off my glasses to rub off the fingerprint Piper accidentally just made over my right eyeball. "All anyone in our grade can talk about is Zooey."

"Well, it's the biggest thing that's happened *all year*," Fee says too loudly as I put my glasses back on and blink her into focus.

"Not everyone's talking about it," Celeste says from the other side of Fee, pulling out her earbud, and then doing the same for Fee. Celeste's bright silver astronaut-looking BMX helmet is perched on top of her head, ready to be tugged down into place. With all the drama at lunch, I'd forgotten how nervously giddy Celeste seemed to be earlier in the day, announcing to our squeals that she was skipping ice time today *and* tomorrow for the festival. She'd make it up on Sunday, she'd said with a gulp, even though it means she'll have to miss church.

"Is that bothering you? That thing with Zooey?" Piper asks, linking her arm with mine and giving it a squeeze. "You've been acting funny since lunch."

I look at her in shock. "Of course it bothered me!" I say, so loudly that a couple of boys from the soccer team look over as they walk by. I flush and lower my voice. "It was awful!"

"It's *middle school*!" Fee says emphatically, like that explains everything.

Piper sighs. "Is that why you keep talking about it, Hattie?"

"ME?!" I squeak, surprised. "I'm not talking about it!" My mind whirs. In every class we went to after lunch, people were talking about what happened with Zooey. But I wasn't! I was just listening. And maybe asking a couple of questions to make sure I understood correctly: Did someone see her mom pick her up from the front office, or was it the guidance office? Were Teagan and Tess *really* spotted in the girls' bathroom after lunch and was one of them maybe really crying? Were they later spotted in the principal's office? Or were they just walking by?

"Yeah, right, you weren't talking about it!" Fee practically screeches, and this time even more people look over in our direction. She lowers her voice.

"You've kind of been talking about it all day, Hattie," Celeste says, not *exactly* unkindly but not all sunshine and lollipops, either.

Fee wrinkles her brow at me. "Didn't this stuff happen in"—she lowers her voice to a faux-tough-girl growl—"Brooklyn?"

"I guess . . . I mean, I'm sure it did." I falter, standing up and slipping on my backpack, embarrassed to realize they're right. I *have* been obsessing about what happened to Zooey all day, but that's just because it is so awful! I have an icky feeling in my belly then, like all of a sudden I realize I've been eating all of that gossip instead of listening to it, and now I have gossip indigestion.

Everything was different in Brooklyn. *I* was different. "There were popular kids at my old school," I finally offer, turning back to face my friends, "but the school was so big, I guess it didn't really matter?" I don't know why I say this as a question, but thinking back to my school in Brooklyn has me feeling sort of wistful and sad. "Everyone just sort of did their own thing."

"Yeah, but what was *your* own thing? Like, what would you and your friend Rae do?" Celeste asks, looking up at me as I stand awkwardly in front of them. I flush, wondering if she somehow knows that I never played organized sports until I moved here, or that my usual thing was reading fantasy books and crocheting mythical creatures on a blanket in the grass at the park with Rae. Or that we succeeded in wearing only T-shirts with cats on them for an entire year of school.

They are all looking at me with interest now and I shrug, looking away. "Same things you do here. You know, sports. And stuff."

"Anyway," Piper says as they stand up and sling on their own backpacks. Celeste gets her bike from where it's leaning behind the bench, and we follow the noisy tangle of kids out of the courtyard. "Forget about the mess with Zooey. She'll be *fine*. There are a ton of other groups that will take her in."

"She could sit with us," Celeste says, getting on her bike but not pedaling, just coasting along with us, parting rivers of colorful fallen leaves as she does. We move down the sidewalk that follows our school's tree-lined driveway toward Main Street, more crowded with kids today because of the cancellation of sports, their unspent energy making them tumbly and loud like puppies.

"No, thanks!" Piper says, shaking her head. "I'm sorry for what happened to her, but that doesn't mean I want her sitting at our table. I mean, can you imagine?" Piper says, shuddering. "Her just sitting there, *staring* at you?"

"She wouldn't sit with us anyway," Fee says. "That would be like a three-rung drop. She'll sit with Izzie Lin and those kids."

"Whatever," Piper says pointedly to Fee. "All I'm saying is, she has options." She looks to our right down the grassy slope that flattens into the practice field for field hockey, and she sighs. "You guys have basketball tryouts in a couple of weeks, right?"

"Basketball?" I squeak, trying to hide the there-are-other-sports? panic from my voice.

"Yeah, city girl," Piper teases, "we can't play field hockey in *winter*."

"Wish you could be on the team," Fee says to Celeste.

Celeste shrugs and says, "I *am* on a team, just not the field hockey team."

"I know," Fee says quietly. It is my cue to leave them to their conversation and fall into step beside Piper.

"Do you think Teagan and Tess will get suspended?" I ask Piper.

"I guess so, probably in-school suspension. They won't have to stay home or anything. Someone saw them in the front office during fifth. They violated the No Bully Pact."

"I'd forgotten about that!" I say, now remembering the printed sheet promising we would never bully others, which we all signed in homeroom the first day of school. "I wish that thing had been, like, binding. Like something that would have actually stopped them from being mean."

"How? Somebody slide-tackles them before they can say anything?" She acts this out for me, raising her flat palm above her eyes like she's looking across a crowded room and shouting, "Bully alert!" before lowering her head and running in place, then leaping onto me and just hanging there.

"Like this?" she asks, legs wrapped around me, resting her bony chin on top of my shoulder.

I laugh, bending over a little so she can scramble down. "Kind of?"

"OH MY GOSH!" Piper cries, stopping so suddenly on the sidewalk that we all bump into one another, Celeste's front tire bouncing off the side of my shoe. The remainder of the kids from school pause to see if we're going to keep going.

"Sorry!" Piper says to them. "Move along! Nothing to see here!"

When they've passed, Piper looks at me, eyes wide, and grins.

"What?" I ask.

Piper gives Fee and Celeste a mischievous look. "We should probably tell Hattie that she's going to get jinxed."

Fee breaks into a wide, goofy smile and says slowly, "She totally is, isn't she?"

"It *is* her first festival," Celeste says solemnly. "Perfect time for a Harvest Jinx."

"Wait, what is a Harvest Jinx?" I ask. "I keep hearing people mention it. I thought it was some sort of apple strudel or something!"

Piper cracks up at this. "Oh, you'll wish it was strudel!"

"It is *so* not strudel," Fee says.

"Then what IS it?!" I practically screech.

Together, the three of them recite, *"Make a promise before you think, and you could get a Harvest Jinx!"*

They all look at me, grinning, like they've actually explained something.

I stare at them. "I don't get it," I say flatly.

"Oh, you'll get it all right!" Celeste says. "If you get jinxed."

"Haven't you heard the poem?" Fee asks. "We all learn it in second grade, for the pageant on the common during the festival."

"I didn't grow up here, you know that!" I say, laughing.

"Do *you*?" Celeste asks, and then she laughs this weird sort of laugh and I'm not exactly sure if it's mean, but it's definitely not friendly.

"Peanut's driving us crazy with practicing!" Piper says, interrupting the strangely tense moment and swatting my *ffftttt* finger away. "She has one line and repeats it a zillion times a day. You haven't heard the poem, ever?"

Peanut is Piper's little sister, the youngest of what Piper calls the Ladies Packenbush, consisting of Piper, her four sisters, and her mom. And get this, the Ladies

Packenbush's home base is one of the stately old Victorian houses that ring the town common, one of the houses that I drooled over when looking at pictures of Trepan's Grove before we moved here.

"Of course I haven't heard the poem! I grew up in—"

"Brooklyn!" Fee interrupts, with her awful imitation.

"Anyway," Piper says excitedly as we start walking again, following the sidewalk's turn down Main Street toward the center of town, "the poem is all about this thing called the Harvest Jinx that says you *have* to keep any promise you make from midnight to midnight the day of the Harvest Festival, or you'll get jinxed."

Just then, a long, shiny pickup truck with GET A GOODY AT GOODY FARMS! stenciled on the side pulls up beside us.

"Fiona," Fee's mom is saying before her window is even rolled all the way down. We all have to look up to see her, because the truck is so darn big. "Hop in. We have a lot of work to do."

The first time I met Fee's mom, I was secretly kind of disappointed. Fee had said her mom's family had been farming the same land for, like, three hundred years and I guess I thought that meant her mom would look like a farmer in a children's story. Overalls, bandanna, hair in braided pigtails. I thought she'd be a warm and cozy sort of person. But instead, I met the woman who is now studying us through the driver's-side window. She has sleek hair and diamond studs and perfect makeup and the long, strong-chinned face that you usually see in ads for Things Rich People Buy. Basically, Fee's mom is what Totally Popular girls turn into when they grow up.

Fee's looks favor her dad more, exactly the sort of cozy, round-faced, dimpled farmer you'd see in one of those baby books with pages so thick you can chew them.

"Fiona! Say your good-byes!" Fee's mom says again, more sharply this time. Her eyes flick over our group, a feeling that raises the little hairs on the back of my neck. Her gaze settles on Celeste and she breaks into a wide smile. "Celestia Martin, Future Olympian! So nice to see you!"

"Hi, Mrs. Goody," Celeste says politely. "Nice to see you, too."

"How is our gold-medalist-in-training today?" Mrs. Goody asks.

Piper makes a *harumph* sound beside me. We've discussed the fact that Mrs. Goody would probably like us better if we were either rich or on track to represent our country in the Olympic Games. "She should see me juggle," Piper whispers beside me, and I stifle a giggle.

"Skating's fine, Mrs. Goody," Celeste says.

"Well, keep at it," Mrs. Goody says. "Not everyone has the body for—"

"Okay. Meet you guys at the Dentist's House tomorrow morning?" Fee interrupts, shooting her mom a look.

"Yep, nine a.m. sharp!" Piper says cheerfully.

"Let us give you a ride home, Celestia," Fee's mom says. "You can put your bike in the back. I'm sure your mom wouldn't want you riding around town with all of these delivery trucks lumbering around."

"Thanks, Mrs. G!" Celeste says.

Piper and I wave good-bye as the truck pulls away, and then Piper says, "So . . . you know how Fee used to ice-skate, too?"

"Yeah. Why'd she stop?"

Piper sighs. "She said she didn't have time for it, but honestly? I think her mom made her stop. Not directly, but . . ."

"How'd she do that?" I ask, even though the sinking feeling in my belly tells me I know the answer.

"Last year Fee kept making all these comments about herself, really mean stuff, about how she was bigger than all the other girls on the skating team and she was going to break through the ice. And even though she'd say that stuff in front of her mom, her mom would never correct her. Never be like, *Don't be dumb, you're not fat* or *So what if you're not the same size, if you love to skate, you should skate.*

She'd just sit there and raise her eyebrows. And then when Fee decided to quit, she told her mom and her mom was like, *Maybe it's for the best, dear. You're built more for field sports, anyway.*"

"That's awful," I say quietly.

"Yep," Piper says. "I think that's why I sometimes give Fee a pass when she says mean stuff. Like, I don't think she has a mean spirit, I think she just picked up some prickliness from her mom."

I think about this as Piper and I round the last bend into the center of town. That's when we see what Mrs. Goody meant about there being a lot of traffic: The grassy town common is lined with delivery trucks, and we watch as teams of four quickly slide out flattened wood booths and lay them in rows on the common, to be set up later.

"Want to come to the Trading Post?" I ask. "I need a Fizzy Fuzz to wash out the taste of Mrs. Goody being a baddy."

Piper checks the time on her phone. "OOH! I can't. The Ladies Packenbush are descending soon! And Peanut and I need to finish booby-trapping our rooms so they can't take them over," she says excitedly, laughing as I poke her in the side. *"Ffftttt!"*

Piper and Peanut are the only two Packenbush girls still living at home. The next two oldest are twins, Paola and Petra. They're both in their first year of college. And the oldest sister, Periwinkle, lives in Manhattan. All three are coming back to Trepan's Grove to see Peanut perform in the pageant.

"Pipes, I am seriously excited about meeting your sisters."

Piper beams and takes in an almost shuddery breath. "I love it when we're all home, but I get so excited I get nervous. Look . . ." She gives me one of her palms. "It's clammy!" I touch her palm, and she's right. She snatches it back with a giggle. "Sorry, that was gross!"

"Well, I still can't wait to meet your sisters," I say as we both wipe our hands on the legs of our pants.

"Unfortunately," Piper says, sighing, "you're going to meet Bruce with the Boat, too."

"Oh," I respond, not sure what else to say. Bruce with the Boat is Piper's mom's boyfriend. He lives in a little brown house on the town pond. I know this because I glimpsed it over the edge of a splintery rowboat the four of us rented from the town boat club late this summer, specifically for the purpose of rowing near his house. Then we had to hit the deck because he chose that moment to walk out on his porch.

"*Oh* is right," Piper says. "He's making us go out on his stupid boat on Sunday."

"Of *course* he is," I say, patting her back.

"But then we're supposed to have dinner with my dad

right after and . . ." She wipes her palms on her pants again. "Ugh. I hope Bruce's stupid boat springs a leak."

"Me too. I hate his boat. His boat is the WORST."

"It would be easier to not like him if he wasn't so nice." Piper groans. I pause as she wipes her eyes with the cuff of her sweatshirt. I hadn't realized she was so upset.

"Pipes . . ." I say.

"It's fine!" she says quickly, stepping back, a watery smile flinching across her face. "Walk me home? Race ya!"

Chapter Five

I still have time after racing Piper home to make a quick stop at the Trading Post before I go meet my dad at the Dentist's House. The Trading Post is as adorable as Mom said it would be. It's a small place with creaky wooden floors, old tin signs for SODA 5 CENTS up on the walls, and a whole back wall lined with bins of penny candy. I stay true to Dad's no-candy-on-weekdays rule, and instead reach for the last raspberry Fizzy Fuzz, shivering when the cold air tunnels through the gap in my sweatshirt cuff and chills my whole arm up to my armpit. Just as my fingers are about to slip around the familiar bottle, someone reaches over me and totally brazenly ganks my drink.

Glowering down at me is a severe-looking dark-skinned girl with an enviable chin cleft and cat's-eye glasses. She has a punk haircut, with blunt bangs cut straight across her forehead, and the rest of her hair cut so short it's practically shaved. She wears a T-shirt with a painting of a woman who has soft lines of hair above her upper lip. Above the picture is handwritten *Unironic Mustache*.

"Um . . ." I step aside so she can close the cooler door.

"*Um* what?" she asks. Her voice is lower—and much louder—than I expected. I watch as she uses the hem of her T-shirt to grip the cap on the bottle of Fizzy Fuzz and twist it off. She lifts the bottle to her lips and takes a long drink, keeping her eyes on me.

"Nothing," I say with a sigh. I look back at the fridge to see what's left.

"Hold on," she baritones when she finally pulls the now half-empty bottle away from her mouth. She swallows a fizzy burp. Her voice is strange, like she's forcing it to be lower than it is. Reflexively, I widen my throat and tuck my chin, trying to imagine what it would feel like to have a voice that low. "Were you reaching for this?" She holds the bottle out to me.

"Yeah, but it's okay," I respond.

She shakes her head gravely. "I have tunnel vision when it comes to refreshments. I'm sorry." She yanks open the refrigerator and pulls out a strawberry Fizzy Fuzz. "Here," she says, opening it with her shirt hem and handing it to me. "It's the next-best flavor."

I look toward the counter at the far end of the store. "Shouldn't we pay . . ."

"It's on me. I run a tab here." And then in the same breath, she bellows, "TRUDY!"

I cringe as the strange girl holds up her drink, and the woman behind the counter looks up. "TIMES TWO!" Trudy nods, pulls a pen from behind her ear, scribbles something down on a piece of paper Scotch-taped to the counter, and then goes back to reading her magazine. The girl looks back to me, satisfied.

"Oh. Okay. Thanks," I say, taking a sip as she watches me and nods.

She just keeps watching and nodding, so I just keep drinking and drinking until I think I might pop, and then I pull the bottle away from my lips, a sickly sweet taste lingering in my mouth. "I'm Hattie," I say, since she's still looking at me and nodding.

"I'M MAUDE," she booms. "Has it left you relatively unscathed, Hattie?"

I don't know how to answer because I don't really know what she's asking. I lift the bottle to my lips but can't bring myself to take another sip when I already have a half bottle fizzing and popping in my belly.

"It's taken your tongue," she growls quietly. "I understand. It stole mine, too."

"What . . . what stole your tongue?" I ask, totally confused.

She raises her chin and says gravely, "Childhood."

The only thing I can think to say is "I'm not a child."

She nods slowly, like I'm proving her point. "You are, though. In the eyes of the law, you are one of your parents' extremities. They *own* you. Until you turn eighteen and can amputate yourself and be free."

"Gross," I say, grimacing.

"How old are you?" Maude asks, and I really don't know how to get out of this conversation, so I answer.

"Twelve."

"Twelve!" She tsks and asks breathlessly, "Is it awful? It's awful, isn't it? How are you holding up?"

"Um, fine, I guess? Probably because I'm Lower Medium Popular." My jaw drops. Why in the world would I say that out loud?

"Riiiight." She makes it obvious that she doesn't believe this is any guarantee of happiness. She stares at me through her cat's-eye frames. "It's all sunshine and lollipops and best friends forever."

Before I can stop myself, I blurt out, "Zooey Dutchman Zervos was publicly defriended in front of the whole cafeteria and it was the most terrible thing I've ever seen in my entire life."

Maude sucks in a breath and winces, like what I've just said is so sad it physically pains her. "Childhood," she says gravely, "is a *wound*."

My lips fall open in shock and I think, *I'm going to laugh*. And then I think, *Don't laugh! She'll eat you alive!* But I just might *have* to laugh because this moment is so weird that if I don't laugh, I might cry.

"It is a wound," she growls on, "that you will spend the rest of your life trying to heal. Do your future self a favor and cauterize the damage now. These childhood lacerations . . . they fester." She thumps her chest, right on the mustached woman's face. "*Inside* of you."

I don't feel like laughing anymore. Suddenly being Lower Medium Popular doesn't seem like much protection against the festering wounds of childhood, especially considering that Zooey was Totally Popular and look what happened to her!

Maude reaches out and, for a second, I think she's going to either pick my nose or give me a noogie, but instead she gently slides my glasses off my face, which, if you don't know, is about the most personal-space-invasive thing you can do to a bespectacled person, and proceeds to polish them with her T-shirt while I blink at her. Then she slips my now clean glasses over my ears and says, "Thank you." Then she turns on her heel and walks toward the back of the store.

chapter six

F*lip.*

Flop.

Twist.

Turn.

UGH!

This is why Mom and Dad always told me not to talk to strangers when they sent me to the bodega on the corner in Brooklyn to pick up milk or pickles, because I might have ended up talking to a *supremely weird* teenager who would make me rethink the entire nature of childhood.

By the time I give up on sleep, it's eleven thirty p.m. and I've kicked off my covers and am lying crosswise on my bed, the bare soles of my feet resting against the cool of the wall, my head hanging off the side, dangerously close to whatever monsters might be hiding in the darkness under my bed.

I reach over to my lamp.

It's still weird to turn on my light in the middle of the night and find myself in my bedroom in Trepan's Grove. I mean, *any* actual bedroom would feel big to me, since my bedroom in our Brooklyn apartment was technically a closet with a window.

Our place in Trepan's Grove is a whole house, just for us. Well, sort of. It's a town house. A town house is like a regular house that's been smooshed in on either side, making it tall and skinny. It's connected paper-doll-style to a line of six other identical town houses, each with woodsy-looking brown shingles and forest-green shutters that hang neat and pretty but don't actually shut. There is a sort of elbow in the very middle of the row of town houses, forming a triangular front parking area hemmed with boxwood and holly bushes. Mom says they'll have bright red berries when winter comes. Our complex is up a narrow wooded road on what people call the far side of town, which means far from the common and the center of town and all of the rich people.

In my old technically-a-closet room, almost the whole space was taken up by the queen-size futon cushion on the floor, colorful pillows propped up along the wall, Rae's old *Frozen* sleeping bag rolled in its place of honor in the corner. My things were all neatly stacked on shelves or hung on hooks that we raised a couple times a year as I grew, to keep me from shish-kebabbing an eyeball.

Childhood is a wound. Maude's words keep echoing in my head, seeming more ominous in these dimly lit, small hours of the night. I give a little shiver and pull Champ into my lap. He forgives me for waking him, shuts his one good eye and purrs blissfully. Dad says Champ is the most pampered cat in the world, but I think he deserves it. The lady at the animal shelter said that he was found outside a coffee shop called Champion one rainy winter morning. He was totally soaked and shaking, mewing pitifully, his right eye so wounded that the vet at the animal shelter wasn't able to save it. I squeeze Champ closer and kiss his head, the same way I always do when I think of him out there, cold and soaking wet and totally alone.

For some reason, the look on Zooey's face today, when the Ts defriended her, flashes before my eyes. She wasn't cold and wet, but she was most definitely alone. If that can happen to people who have been friends since they were in diapers, what hope is there for a friendship that's only a few months old?

What guarantee is there that the same thing can't happen to me? That I won't be the one dodging verbal daggers flung by my friends?

The horrible thing is, there isn't a guarantee.

I mean, not really. Just like the No Bully Pact we all signed on the first day of school, friendship isn't really a binding contract.

But what if . . . what if it was?

I reach over, nudging Champ off my lap, and jiggle the drawer in my bedside table until it squeaks open. I pull out a notebook and pen. I slip out of bed and onto the soft carpet, open the notebook to the first page, and tap my pen at the top, thinking. Finally, I write *THE FRIENDSHIP PACT.*

It takes me a moment to figure out where to start, but finally I begin:

We, the undersigned, promise . . .

I write until my hand hurts, until it's past midnight. I write the last part with my heavy head resting on my arm, at eye level with my notebook, drawing four lines at the bottom. I read back over what I wrote and then sign my name on the top line. I fall asleep there, on the floor, feeling like I've done something important. If my friends will agree, it's a guarantee.

chapter seven

S LOW DOWN!" my mom calls even before I skid around the corner into the kitchen the next morning. She's towering over the juicer on the counter, her blond curly hair up in a bun, her green scrubs freshly ironed and hanging like dry cleaning on her wiry frame.

Mom glances up to smile at me as she shoves a carrot down the juicer's gullet. "Want some juice?" she asks. I grimace as the carrot comes out the little silver spout, reduced to orange goop not unlike the cheese crackers in Zooey's mouth yesterday.

"No, thanks," I say, backing away dramatically until I'm leaning against the refrigerator. I reach behind me and open the freezer door and pull out a box of waffles to hold in front of myself like a shield. "That stuff looks radioactive."

"Radioactively *awesome*!" my dad says, strutting into the kitchen and stretching up to kiss my mom on the cheek. My dad's big brothers tease him about marrying someone taller than he is every time we see them, playful jabs called across the table in the same breath they use to ask for more Parmesan or to insist that one of my little cousins eat his escarole. *Sal, you still standing on your tiptoes so your wife doesn't see how short you are? Hattie, whack your cousin on the back; I think she's choking. There you go. It's out. It was an olive. Thanks, doll.*

My dad doesn't seem to mind the teasing; he always comes back with something like, *Aw, you're just jealous my girl can dunk!*

Yeah, dunk you in her coffee like biscotti!

And it goes on like that through dessert.

"*Ew*, Dad!" I squeal, taking in the Boston Red Sox shorts that hang huge on his compact frame. "Nobody wants to see the town dentist's knobby knees on a Saturday morning!"

"What?" he asks in mock offense, looking down at his clothes. "These are *sport shorts!*"

I crack up at how thick his Boston accent has gotten since he moved back to his home state. "Spot shots?" I tease.

"Hey!" he says, taking the box of waffles from me and popping a couple into the toaster. "My glorious diction"— he plays up the Boston accent—"was deep undercover for ten years in pinstripe territory."

"Pinstripes?" I ask in mock confusion. "You don't mean . . ."

"Don't you name those turkeys in my house!"

"You mean the New York Yank—"

I squeal and duck as my dad flings a waffle in my general direction.

"And don't tease me about my shorts!" Dad says. "You're a jock now. You got sport shorts of your own!"

"Stop saying 'sport shorts'!" I laugh, bending over to pick up the waffle from under the kitchen table, blowing the germs off it, and handing it to my dad so he can put it in the toaster. "That one's yours. And I'm not a jock."

Mom crams a rib of celery into the juicer. "Your stinky field hockey uniform waiting for you to wash it begs to differ."

She takes a second look at my outfit. "And speaking of uniforms . . ."

"Mom!" I exclaim, a little hurt.

She gasps a little when she sees my face, turns off the groaning juicer, and strides over to wrap an arm around my shoulder and give me a squeeze. "Oh, I'm sorry, honey, you look great. I just miss the times you wore something other than cords and a stripy sweatshirt and Converse."

"This is just what people wear here," I say with a small shrug, even though I understand what she means. I *am* getting kind of tired of wearing the same sort of thing every day.

"I get it," Mom says, giving me another squeeze. "I was twelve once, too." For some reason, this makes me touch my front right pocket, where my top secret project from last night, the carefully folded Friendship Pact, is waiting to be signed by my friends. I wrap my arms around my mom and hug her.

"Stop the lovey stuff and eat your breakfast, ya jock!" Dad says with a grin, putting my waffle on a plate and wrapping his in a napkin before heading toward the stairs. "We're out of here in five."

"Put some pants on!" I holler after him.

My friends are waiting for me on the wide front porch of the Dentist's House, just like we'd planned, and before I'm even out of my dad's car they are yelling, "HATTIE!" and I am calling back, "I'M HERE!" and then I fake limp up the steps and across the porch and we all hug and squeal and jump around and my dad calls us goofballs.

He reminds us he'll be open today for Candy Apple Related Tooth Emergencies, so we can come back if we want to take a breather or use the bathroom or floss the cotton candy off our teeth. Luckily, he goes inside before he can offer any more embarrassing suggestions.

"So should we go?" Piper asks excitedly, looking across the street to where the common is already flooded with people. The colorful booths are all set up, the town band is playing a cheerful tune at the base of the Chin statue, and behind them is the empty stage where Peanut and her class will perform in the pageant. I see cotton candy and balloons and a lady on stilts, and on the far side of the common a long line of people board a school bus hung with the banner FREE SHUTTLE TO GOODY FARMS U-PICK APPLE ORCHARD.

"This is going to be the best day ever," Celeste says, reading my mind. We all start moving toward the steps, when I remember what's in my pocket.

"Wait," I say, suddenly nervous. "Before we go over, I have something first." I pull out the folded piece of paper.

"What is it?" Fee asks, reaching out to pluck it from my hand. Celeste leans over to look, and Piper stoops over so she can read out loud. "'The Friendship Pact.' What the heck?"

I take the paper back, suddenly unsure. "It's . . . it's just a . . ."

"Is this about what happened with Zooey?" Piper sighs.

I gulp. "Sort of. I just thought . . . maybe . . ."

"Can I see?" Celeste asks, waiting for me to hand it to her. I do, and lean against the railing as she reads aloud:

THE FRIENDSHIP PACT

We, the undersigned, promise to never lie to each other, share each other's secrets, gossip about each other, or fight in a public place.

"Wait. Hold on. Hattie, you really think we need this?" Piper asks, looking at me after hearing the first sentence, and sounding a little hurt.

"No, it was just a dumb idea," I say, taking it back from Celeste before she can keep reading. Hot tears prick at my eyes.

"Wait," Fee says, taking the paper from me. She surprises me by saying, "Maybe it's *not* such a bad idea."

"Really?" Celeste asks hotly. "You think without this piece of paper, we would turn on each other? We never needed it before . . ." She gives me a hard stare, and I look away.

Piper says, "No way! But . . . I mean . . . if it would make Hattie feel better."

"All I ask," Fee says with a dimpled grin, "is that I get to choose the consequence."

Celeste huffs and shakes her head. "Whatever. I'll sign it if it means that much to you guys." I can tell from her voice that *you guys* does not include me.

Fee gives an evil-sounding laugh and pulls a pen from her I GOT A GOODY AT GOODY FARMS tote bag. She works quietly for a bit, kneeling on the porch floor, moving the paper now and again to keep the pen from poking through between the boards. Finally, she sits up and says, "It's all done. Let's sign it."

"Me first!" Piper says, and I smile.

THE FRIENDSHIP PACT

We, the undersigned, promise to never lie to each other, share each other's secrets, gossip about each other, or fight in a public place.

If any one of us does any of the things above, the others will basically forget she ever existed until amends are made.

One by one, they add their names to the lines under mine.

My friends skim right by the very first booth we get to when we step onto the crowded common, but I stop. The booth is occupied by an elegant-looking woman leaning over the little table in front of her, carefully arranging her wares.

I blink at them, not sure I am seeing correctly.

"Are those . . ." I ask, coming closer. "Are those from Tilde's Realm?" I ask, taking in the crocheted faerie creatures standing in neat rows. She has them on a tablecloth printed with things you would find on a map—forests, mountain ranges, lakes.

The woman in the booth seems to grow taller as she grins, her long neck stretching as her back straightens. She nods first, then answers. "They are."

"Wow," I whisper, picking up a gyrgone, a small, cat-like creature with a sharp beak that allows it to burrow in through your belly button. I step back to take in the way she has all the creatures set up. "It's like they're lined up for battle, but they wouldn't really be together, right?" I say. The woman smiles as I continue. "Because they're all from different realms, so they wouldn't be in, like, the same place at the same time. I mean, the link between the realms was closed, right? So there's no way they would be together." I'm babbling, but it's been so long since I've talked to any-one about Tilde's Realm that it feels nice to be doing it now. "Wait. Do you think that's what's going to happen in the last book? That the portals between the realms will open?" I blink at her, imagining it. "That would be awesome."

She laughs. "That *would* be awesome." She nods as I hold up my phone, asking for permission to snap a photo. I do, and send it to Rae.

"They say Calliope Zehra is going to blow everyone away with the last book," I add, and I'm about to ask where she stands on the witches versus faeries controversy from book two, but then my friends trot over, arms twined in a three-link chain that looks startlingly whole without me.

"Ooooh, what are these!" Piper squeals, picking up a one-horned phylcoscent. "Is this one a unicorn?"

"Not a unicorn!" the woman and I object at the same time, and we exchange a grin before I twist it back into my mouth. She explains, "Common mistake. In the realm, it is said, 'Call a phylcoscent a unicorn, and discover the sharpness of her horn.'"

"Ohmygod, these are those bizarro creatures from that book series the indoor kids are always reading!" Fee says, roughly handling a dew faerie.

Celeste gasps, points at Fee. "Rude! Apologize to the lady!"

Fee huffs, points back at Celeste, and says, "Bossy!" but she does turn to the woman behind the booth and say, "Sorry."

The woman says nothing to her, but gently removes the faerie from Fee's hand, turns to me, and asks, "Would you like to buy one?"

I put the gyrgone down. "No, I haven't actually read the books. Thanks, though."

My phone vibrates with a text back from Rae, giving me an excuse to look away from the woman's confused stare. "I love them! Which did you get?"

My fingers hover over the phone for a second before I write her back. "Gyrgone!"

My phone buzzes again when she texts back, but I slip it into my pocket instead of answering. I don't want to spend the whole day bent over my phone, talking to Rae, instead of actually enjoying the festival.

Piper links elbows with me and tugs, saying, "Come on, Hattie!" and we run until we catch up with Fee and Celeste, and then just for a moment, before the crowd forces us to break apart, we are a chain of four and I am suddenly filled with this giddy happiness that makes my heart feel like it's going to leap straight out of my chest.

And then something weird happens.

I mean, something weird *must* have happened, because the next thing I know, there is this *whooshing* sound and the slam of a car door, and I'm standing on the sidewalk in front of our town house, holding the handles of a small white paper shopping bag. It's getting dark out, and the neighbors' front lights are flicking on one by one. My hand is raised, and I'm waving as Mrs. Goody's red truck eases out of the parking area toward the wooded road. My head is cocked to the side, and the fingers of the hand I'm waving are going loose and folding in as I lock eyes with Piper through the back window. She's waving, too, but her face is an echo of how mine feels. There is her usual smile, but it is slipping from her face, and by the time the station wagon turns and disappears down the wooded road, she is staring at me, her eyebrows crunched together.

"Huh," I say aloud, turning toward our front steps. I glance absently down the row of our town house neighbors. Pumpkins on front steps, decorative wooden scarecrows staked into little front lawns, fall-colored wreaths on the doors. If everything is the same as when I left this morning, why do I feel so *odd*?

I shudder and sniffle, suddenly aware of how cold and damp the air is, like we are about to get an icy rain. I hurry up the steps to our place, anxious to get inside.

"How was the festival?" My mom's voice floats through the front door, along with the scent of something warm and savory and delicious.

"Good?" I answer, keeping my sweatshirt on but kicking my high-tops into the shoe bin.

"Are you getting a cold?" she asks, somehow still unaccustomed to the fact that I am Hattie: Forever Sniffly. She adds, "You had fun?"

Did I have fun? I ask myself as I sock foot it up the steps from the front hall to the first floor. When I try to think of the day, I definitely remember it, but it's like the memories are swirled together into one memory that seems to encompass everything that happened from the moment we left the Tilde's Realm lady 'til I found myself standing outside our house.

In the memory, I am spinning. Laughing hysterically and spinning in a circle, my arms outstretched, my head tipping back from the force of my own rotation. All around me the colors stream like a sideways rainbow, and there is so much *sound*—laughter and music, the clonk and splash of a ball hitting the target on the dunk tank and a varsity soccer player hitting the water, the hiss and rubbery squeal of balloons being filled at helium tanks, the *jingle-hiss-pop-cheer* of "pop the balloon by squirting water in a clown's mouth" games, the crunch of apples, the *click click click* of the photo booth's camera as we all cram in for pictures, the smoosh of gross apple pie in my mouth, and the adorable sounds of Peanut and the other second graders proudly chanting on stage, *Make a promise before you think, and you could get a Harvest Jinx!*

We made plans. I somehow know that, even if I don't really remember the conversation. We are going to meet up before school on Monday. Fee will bring apple cider doughnuts from the farm stand. I'll bring apple tea.

chapter Eight

I yawn my way through dinner, feeling more like myself after having some of my mom's lasagna.

Mom and Dad try to send me to bed early, but since it's Saturday night and I'm a sixth grader, I inform them I am "Yawn. Planning on staying up a bit. Yawn." I finally relent when Dad starts counting my molars every time I yawn. "One, two, three . . ."

"Stay out of my mouth!" I tell him, before bidding them good night.

I grab the paper shopping bag from where I left it at the bottom of the stairs and drag myself up to my room. I summon the strength of champions and manage to brush my teeth, wash my face, *and* put on pj's before I snuggle under the covers. It's then that I peek into the shopping bag, a flood of memories coming back as I take out first one and then another object.

A narrow column of photo-booth pictures. Fee, Piper, Celeste, and me, goofing off, being "serious," being "mature." I remember the feel of Piper's scrawny arm around my shoulders, the light way that Fee perched on my lap when I patted my knee, the soft tickle of Celeste's hair on my cheek. Piper smiled with her mouth closed in the first three, but just before the last one, Fee said, "Let's hurry so we don't miss Peanut!" and I gave Piper a good hard *fffttttt* with my fingertips right in her tickle spot and she burst out laughing. That picture is the best, all of us laughing, Piper's braces glinting, Fee's dimples dimpling, Celeste's chin pointing right at my smile. I set the picture on my nightstand. I'll tuck it in the frame of my mirror tomorrow. Next I pull out a small white waxed bag taped shut with a heart sticker. I slide my finger under the seal and tip the bag, letting a small silver ring slip out into my palm. It is thin as thread, sold as a set of four. We all pitched in, handing our folded bills to Celeste so she could count them and hand them to the man at the booth. I slip it on my pinkie finger. My stomach does a sickly flip-flop when I pull out the last thing. It's a blue ribbon, with printing in gold in its center that reads PIE-EATING CONTEST CHAMPION. JUNIOR DIVISION. I try to focus on how good Mom's dinner tasted tonight as I remember the taste of SO MUCH APPLE PIE.

* * *

As I sleep, I'm vaguely aware of the first few clatter-splats of rain against my window, and when I wake up Sunday morning, the rain is still going, the world grayed and blurred through a thick forest of never-ending bead-ball strands clattering from the sky.

It's a long, cozy day. We turn on the heat and high-five when it doesn't screech and rattle like the radiators we had back in Brooklyn. I do my homework, avoid washing my field hockey uniform, watch nineties action movies with my parents, and eventually give up on texting my friends, who are apparently too busy to text back. I tell myself Celeste will be on the ice all day, and Piper will be with Bruce, but not on the Boat, and then at her dad's. And Fee . . . Well, Fee will be at the farm stand, cleaning up after a day of busloads of tourists coming through. I do get ahold of Rae, but I think she's mad I didn't text her back yesterday. We chat a little, but my last text to her goes unanswered.

The rain stops during the night but leaves the air damp and cold. Dad is bringing me to school early for my doughnut date with the girls, and I wait for him out front to avoid him and Mom telling me I'm going to be too cold in just my stripy sweatshirt.

I spend my wait gingerly picking up waterlogged worms from the sidewalk, their bodies pale and stretched thin, and placing them back in the leaf-covered grass.

Dad gets me to school so early that I'm the first kid in the soaked courtyard, so early that when I glance through the cafeteria window, I see the dark ceiling lights flicker and snap to life, illuminating one of the cafeteria ladies as she walks in, yawns, and takes off her coat. I wipe the wet leaves from a bench with my sweatshirt sleeve and sit on the very edge, listening to the sounds of the chairs being taken off the tables in the cafeteria and slid into place.

I wait a few minutes and then decide to get the tea ready for when Piper, Fee, and Celeste get here. I set my backpack on the bench and open it, pulling out the little tin cups from the tea set I had as a kid. The pink and white flowers painted along the rims are flaked and fading, but I don't care, I still love it. I set the teacups on the bench, all in a row.

Another car comes up the driveway just as I'm pouring steaming hot water from my thermos into the teacups, but it turns out to be a couple of random eighth graders getting dropped off by their dads. Being eighth graders, they barely glance at me as they walk by. I put a tea bag in each cup and glance up to see the cafeteria lady watching me from the window. I look back down, pretending to be interested in the darkening water of the teacups, and wish my friends would get here already.

More cars come, a few with kids from my class. I smile and say hi to them as they pass or as they stake claim on the edges of their own damp benches. Then the buses come and the courtyard becomes flooded with kids. I try to smile as a few girls from class coo, "Oh, those are so cute!" when they see my teacups, and I just gulp and try not to disintegrate when Teagan and Tess scoff in unison, "Aren't we a little *old* for tea parties?"

First bell rings and the courtyard starts to empty, and the tea has steeped so long that the water is now a dark, muddy brown. Second bell rings, and the courtyard really empties. I nod in reply to the kids who ask, "You coming, Hattie?" And then I'm alone in the courtyard again. Where *are* they?!

I end up chugging all four cups of tea because the lunch lady is glaring at me out the window and what if she considers tea dumping littering? I drink it so quickly that some of it dribbles down my chin and soaks the collar of my shirt with apple-scented heat. I hurry into school, my stomach a hot ocean full of sloshing tea.

The locker hall is pretty much empty by the time I dump in my backpack, teacups, and thermos and grab my stuff for first period, language arts with Ms. Lyle. I skid around the corner just as she is about to shut the classroom door. "Watch the clock, please, Ms. Maletti!" she says, her wind-through-dry-leaves voice sharper than usual. She closes the door behind me and walks slowly over to her desk.

"Hey!" I whisper breathlessly, dropping into my seat at the double desk I share with Celeste. "Where *were* you guys?"

Celeste turns and looks at me, pulling out an earbud from beneath her curls. "Excuse me?" Then she wrinkles her nose. "No offense, but you smell very apple-y."

"I know I smell apple-y!" I lay my arm across the smooth, cool wood of the desk, and lay my head on my elbows, trying to catch my breath. "Where *were* you this morning?"

"Um . . . on the ice? And then here." She taps her fingers on the desk. "At this desk." So that's why I didn't see her! Her practice must have run late. But still . . .

"We were supposed to meet!" I say.

Her brow furrows. "Wait, what? Are you new here?" The fact that she says our little inside joke softens the blow just a bit.

A moment later, a shadow falls over our desk. I look up. "Fee!" I say, but she doesn't answer; she just looks at Celeste.

"You cut your bangs!" Celeste and I say at the same time, gaping at the newly shorn, jagged tufts that have replaced the demi-curtain of hair that used to hang over Fee's eyes.

"They're kind of short," Celeste says, almost wincing.

"I did them myself!" Fee says, breaking into a wide, goofy smile.

"So that's what you were doing yesterday," Celeste says, a little icily. I guess I'm not the only person Fee didn't text back. I watch as Fee glances across the room to where Teagan and Tess are. They don't return her gaze. Fee's lips twitch into a tiny, quick pout. Then she looks hard at me. "Friend of yours, Celeste?"

I gasp, stung by the edge in Fee's voice, and Celeste gives me a puzzled look. Then she shrugs and says to Fee, "I think she's new here."

Fee doesn't miss a beat. "Well, newbie, this is my seat. And I'd like to sit in it."

"You guys . . ." I say, a surprised, hurt tone thinning my voice.

"Ladies and gentlemen!" Ms. Lyle's wavery voice manages to quiet the room, and she pushes her thick green-framed glasses farther up the bridge of her nose. "Please take your seats. I want you all to reread the next chapter before we start our close examination of the first paragraph."

"That paragraph is, like, twenty sentences long!" Fee says with a groan, dropping her books in front of me. "Newbie, out of my seat."

"Be polite at least!" Celeste says to Fee. Then to me, "It's her seat. There's a place in the back row."

I stand, but look desperately at Fee and Celeste. "But . . ."

"Thanks," Fee says, moving around me and sitting down. She keeps her eyes forward.

A terrible shudder sends pinpricks over my skin. "Are . . . are you guys mad at me?"

They exchange a befuddled look but don't answer.

"You guys . . ." My voice cracks, I raise my hands lamely, like I might reach out and touch them to make sure they're real.

They completely ignore me. Ms. Lyle doesn't, and asks me to take my seat.

A lump blooms in my throat, and my breath can't move around it. I move clumsily to the only empty seat in class, in the back, clutching my books to my pounding chest.

This has to be a joke, right?

I sit on the edge of my chair, my books still pressed against me, and stare at the backs of their heads as if I could send my brain waves into their skulls and ask them, *Why are you doing this? What did I do? How could we go from having the* best day of our entire lives *at the festival to . . . this?*

They don't even turn their heads to sneak a peek at me. Like they've just forgotten I was even here. How could they not even, you know, check to see if being mean to me had crumbled me to rubble? Isn't that the whole point of being a jerk? To see what damage you can do? I mean, isn't that why Zooey just stands there staring at you while you try not to cry after a drive-by Zooey and the Ts insult attack?

I need to talk to Piper.

And what's worse, we have a double period with Ms. Lyle, which means we go straight from me having to pretend to pay attention to a close examination of *The Giver* to second-period social studies, which means fifty *more* minutes of being ignored by my friends and feeling like I'm going to literally BURST into tears and blow salt water and snot all over everyone.

It is positively *endless*.

This is what I hear as I stare at the illustration of a woman in a pioneer bonnet hanging a black pot over a blazing fire and will myself not to cry. *Blah blah blah colonials blah blah blah Pilgrims blah blah blah quarter projects blah blah blah Zooey and Hattie.*

Wait. What?!

I look up to see Ms. Lyle staring at me, and the rest of the class, even Celeste and Fee, swinging around to stare. Apparently, I said that out loud. "Is there a problem, Hattie?" Ms. Lyle asks in a newspaper-rustle voice.

I shake my head, stealing a glance at Zooey. She looks like a Disney starlet playing a sixth-grade mean girl who is crabby over the fact that she's just been partnered with a total dork. We lock eyes and I sit up straighter, hoping for the sort of posture that sends the message: *Back off, Queen*

Bee. She rolls her eyes and then actually flips her hair, like, *at* me, like a weapon, and turns back toward the front. Darren, the gap-toothed kid who's sitting in front of me, turns to hand me a copy of the assignment that's being passed out. He gives me a sorry half smile to go with it. "No, there's no problem, Ms. Lyle," I say softly.

"Good." Ms. Lyle walks back behind her desk. "You all see on the handout that this research paper is worth one-third"—she says this again—"*one-third* of your grade. I want citations. I want footnotes. I want appendices. Most of all, I want you to *move* me, make me remember why it is I chose to return to Trepan's Grove, the town of my youth, and teach you all social studies. You'll need me to approve your topics. Again, check the handout for the specifics—one page, three paragraphs, on what your topic is, why you've chosen it, and how you plan to research. Topic proposals are due on November first. That is two weeks from this Wednesday, ladies and gentlemen."

And to think I was actually excited about this assignment when I saw it on the syllabus at the beginning of the year. I was going to do Food and Dental Care in Colonial Times. Dad was going to help me make a set of colonial dentistry instruments, which would have been basically a saw and a pair of pliers.

I was secretly hoping I'd get partnered with Jacob, the soccer-playing superstar who has a way of chewing on the white cord of his hooded sweatshirt that makes me swoon. Once, I had to look away really quick because he caught me watching as he accidentally bit off the little plastic part on the end. I didn't look away fast enough, because he saw me and then shrugged like *that was weird* and then he pulled the little plastic bit off the tip of his tongue with his pointer finger and flicked it on the ground. It was the most romantic thing I have ever seen. And I could feel my eyes get really big and I just stared at the little shiny wet spot on the tip of his finger until he wiped it on the side of his soccer shorts.

I reenacted the whole thing for Piper in the orange bathroom in the science wing, and we squealed a bunch and then basically died because OH MY GOD HE LOOKED AT ME WHILE HE TOUCHED HIS TONGUE. "That's, like, basically kissing from a distance," Piper informed me breathlessly before we cracked up and died all over again.

But now . . . Jacob is partnered with Darren, Fee and Celeste are ignoring me, and my stomach is in knots.

I watch the second hand tick around and around, the minute hand in deathly slow pursuit, but when class is finally over, I don't get up. I make myself stay at my desk as the whole class files out, not wanting to go anywhere near Fee and Celeste when they're acting this way. I wait until everyone leaves, even Zooey, who actually pauses to look at me before walking out of the room, like now she's done flipping her hair in my general direction and actually wants to talk about the project. Well, she can't just decide to talk to me after giving me the stink eye from afar all year.

Fee would be ecstatic if she was the one partnered with Zooey. In fact, she kind of lost it at the beginning of the year when the two of them were partnered for this project. Celeste and I were teamed up for the same project, and we both assumed that we'd meet with Fee and Zooey and all work together. But Fee was like no, we need to work just with our teams. Which left Celeste and me in that weird situation where you hang out with someone you're not usually alone with. I thought it might bond us, but Celeste remained as nice-but-not-too-nice as she's always been.

But Fee was *so* excited, she even made cupcakes. *You know, in case she's hungry,* she explained. But the next day when we saw her, Fee reluctantly admitted that the Ts had shown up with Zooey, and Zooey spent the whole time talking to them. Fee ended up doing most of the work herself while they ate all her cupcakes. *But they were really nice!* Fee said. *They didn't make fun of me at all. I mean, Zooey's mom and my mom have known each other since child-hood, so we go, like, way back.* Zooey and the Ts called Fee Cupcake after that, and she would dimple up like it was some kind of compliment. It wasn't. Because the first time

Zooey called her Cupcake, Teagan muttered, "As in, have another."

Once the coast is clear, I go straight to the lunchroom, not even grabbing my lunch bag. Piper's teacher always lets her out a few minutes earlier than Ms. Lyle does, so she's always there waiting for us, the ONLY NUT ALLOWED sign propped up in place.

"Oh my gosh," I say, tears already choking my voice as I sit down next to Piper. I take a shuddering breath, ready to tell her all about what happened, when she turns and looks at me.

Her blank face takes my breath away.

"Pipes?" I croak.

She smiles. "Have we met? Are you new here?"

I suck in my lips and stand up, almost tipping the bench out from under Piper as I do. "Please don't do this," I say.

She looks honestly confused. "Do what?"

"Piper . . ." I say, my voice choked, pleading.

"Oh, wait, please don't cry!" she says, her eyes welling up with tears. "I have contagious—"

"Contagious crying syndrome, I know!" I practically wail. "Piper, what is going on?"

"I don't know how you know my . . ." She falters, then seems to regroup. "It's going to be okay!" Piper says, swallowing back tears. "I think maybe you just came to the wrong lunch period or something. Can you go to the front office? They'll look at your schedule."

I back away, scanning the cafeteria, horrified when I see that other people have turned their attention to me. I turn quickly and focus on the entrance at the far end of the cafeteria. I don't look at anybody when I walk, not even Dr. Schroeder, who must have seen what happened because she's holding out a hall pass for me as I hurry by.

Mr. Zubki, the school librarian, stares down the hawkish slope of his nose as I stammer out my request to eat in the school library. I liked Mr. Zubki from the start, at first just because he wore old-man clothes even though he's young, and then because he wouldn't comment when you asked him to help you find books about *growing up, like, um, getting older and more, um, mature* when obviously you were hoping for books that have titles like *Where Are My Boobs?* and *First, Create a Distraction: Tips for Smuggling Lady Products into the Bathroom So No One Knows You Have Your Period.* He would just tell you what section to look in.

I am hot-faced and nodding and trying not to cry as Mr. Zubki says, "Sure, Hattie. Everything okay?" He takes my almost frantic nod for a positive answer and says I can stay. I turn on my heel and rush away. I know it's rude not to say thank you, but I also know that I don't want to sob all over his desk.

I head straight for the Big Comfy Chair, the cartoonish poufy chair that sits facing a long picture window along the back wall of the library. In front of the chair is a shaggy rug and about a dozen floppy pillows, making it the perfect nook for after-school study sessions before field hockey practice. And now it's going to be the perfect place for me to flop facedown and quietly cry my eyes out and maybe consider calling my mom to come pick me up, because what happened today has to be just as bad as throwing up at school.

But when I come up to the back of the chair, a sob finally squeaking from my throat, I see it's already occupied. Someone's combat boots are slung over one arm, and I manage to veer away into the stacks before whoever it is can sit up and catch a glimpse of me. The chair cushions make their singular *sigh* sound as whoever it is lies back down.

I wander around the library for a couple of minutes, annoyed that when they built this bright, beautiful place, they didn't consider the bookish kids who might need a place to hide and cry. It's not until I settle into the very last computer carrel that I realize I don't even have my lunch.

I don't call mom to come pick me up. I just power through the rest of the day.

She's in our little front yard when I get home, her long, curly hair tucked under a red bandanna tied at the nape of her neck. "Hey, Hattie," she says, sitting back on the heels of her work boots to greet me. Her cheeks are flushed from the chilly air and her hard work. "I'm putting in some bulbs before the first frost. Want to help?"

I force a smile. "Hi, Mom. No, I have homework."

"No field hockey today?" she asks, leaning a little so she can watch me trudge up the front steps.

My shoulders drop as I realize I just left school without even telling Ms. Thackary I wasn't coming to field hockey practice. Now I'm going to be in trouble with her, too. "Too much homework," I say again as I open the door. "Academics first, remember?" I say, echoing Mom and Dad's condition for me signing up for the field hockey team with my friends.

I don't hear her response because I close the door behind me.

In my room, I dump my backpack and sweatshirt on the floor and flop onto my bed. Champ rolls off my pillow, stretching his full length on his back, reaching his nose over to touch mine.

"Oh, Champ," I say, fat tears rolling down my face. I'm not really a cry-your-eyes-out type person. I usually start to get bored after a few minutes, and then I start to worry about dehydration.

But this time I cry until all I have left are hiccups, and then I sniffle and hiccup my way through a snack of Skittles I had hidden under my bed for emergencies like this.

I know I should go outside and tell Mom what happened, but the thought of admitting what just happened—I can't. I can't bear to hear my mom gently say, *Hattie, we told you that the friendship was moving a little fast.* Because they did. They did tell me.

I turn over on my stomach and then squirm as something presses against me. I reach into my pocket and pull out a folded piece of paper. The corners have rounded and softened, and when I unfold it, the creases stay. I put it on my bed in front of me and smooth it with my palm to get it to lay flat.

The Friendship Pact.

I bet this is the reason my friends are acting so awful. They're mad I came up with this, mad I made them sign it. Why did I ever think it was a good idea? I would have never asked Rae to sign something like that. I glance down at my backpack, thinking about how I could get out my phone and text Rae right now. Tell her how everything is going wrong, and ask her what I should do. But I realize I kind of blew off her texts during the Harvest Festival, and she really didn't seem to want to talk yesterday. I don't think I could handle reaching out to her and having her ignore me. I can't totally fail at all my friendships in one day.

Do Piper and the others think I did something to break the pact? My stomach lurches at the thought.

"But I didn't DO anything!" I say desperately to Champ, who flicks his tail at me. At least, I don't think I did. The Harvest Festival is a total blur. I hold the paper limply in my hand, the last few days running through my mind like a movie.

Did I lie? No.

Gossip? No.

All I did, I think tearfully, was get my best friends to sign a piece of paper saying that we would always be best friends and that we would never do something exactly like what they're doing today. We promised. And now they are acting like they've forgotten me.

Wait.

Forgotten. Promised. Forgotten. Promised. What is it about those words? *Promise, promise . . .*

I leap off the bed. "MAKE A PROMISE BEFORE YOU THINK, AND YOU COULD GET A HARVEST JINX!"

chapter Nine

Jinxed?!

I drop the pact like it's on fire and leap away, pointing at it from across the room, yelling, "NO WAY!"

Champ licks his speckled nose and yawns his cat-lion yawn, totally unconcerned with the fact that the whole world may just have gone completely bananas.

"Don't panic," I whisper to Champ, staying very still for a moment, trying to stop this awful possibility from going any further. My ears feel swollen with the sound of my own heartbeat, and a tingly feeling sweeps up and down my entire body. "Not happening," I whisper. "Not happening."

I get out my phone.

My finger pauses over Piper's name. *Please know me*, I think, *please please please know who I am.*

"Piper?" I ask tentatively when she answers. "It's Hattie."

"Hattie?" she asks, the same blank voice as this morning.

"Yes. Hattie," I say firmly. "Your best friend."

"I'm sorry, I . . ."

"You know me, Piper. Remember, we met at the town pond in July? You bought me a purple Popsicle and your little sister took a giant bite of it when I sat down on your beach towel."

Piper laughs. "That's totally something Peanut would—"

"*Ffftttt!*" I say quickly, hoping the sound will jog her memory.

"Bless you?" she says uncertainly. And then, "Sorry, but I don't really remember—"

"I'm tall, Piper, and I have short, curly hair and I wear glasses and I'm afraid of things with more or less than two legs and I help you with math and you help me with Spanish and—"

"Wait!"

I stop talking, hold my breath.

"Are you the new girl from lunch today at school?"

"You remember me?"

"Yeah, you sat down next to me and started crying. Are you okay?"

I frantically scan my room, looking for something my eyes can rest on that will calm me, and I catch sight of the strip of photo-booth pictures we took at the festival.

"Piper?" I ask, my voice shaking.

"Yeah?"

"What did you do on Saturday?" I walk slowly toward my mirror. A sudden rain bats against the windows. I hear my mom stomping her boots, laughing, saying, "Whew!" as the front door closes.

"I went to the festival," Piper says. "Why?"

I pull the strip of photos from the mirror frame and stare at them. "Who did you go with?"

"Who did I go with to the festival? My friends Celeste and Fee. Why?"

"No reason," I say softly, already pressing END on the phone.

I stare hard at the pictures.

In them, I am alone.

chapter ten

Break the jinx, break the jinx, break the stupid jinx!

My lips twitch with these words streaming through my head as I sit ramrod straight on the bus on the way to school, my fingers gripping the edge of the nubbly vinyl seat. I'm too anxious to even take off my backpack. Last night was endless and awful, mostly because I stuck with my decision not to tell my mom and dad about the jinx. And you know what? I do NOT like keeping things from my mom and dad. I mean, I used to read my diary entries out loud at breakfast! I am going to be terrible at being a secretive teenager. I do know a girl's got to have her secrets. Like the fact that sometimes I raid the cookies Mom hides in the prehistoric box of Vegetable Medley she brought with us from Brooklyn for the precise reason of hiding things in the back of the freezer. Or that some-times I like to rock in the chair on the front porch of the Dentist's House and imagine being an action hero and saving the world. Or that sometimes I practice kissing on my pillow, except not French kissing because that leaves a drool spot and drool is gross, which may present a problem when I participate in actual kissing. Parents really don't need to know about those things. But being forgotten by my friends? That's the kind of secret that gives me a sour, prickly feeling in my stomach, the kind of secret you're supposed to tell your parents before the sour, prickly feeling eats you up.

And I will tell them.

Later.

Unless my plan works today, and then I'll never have to think about the stupid jinx again.

I barely slept last night, but I'm not even really tired.

Well, maybe I'm a little tired. Just like in that part of my brain above my left eyebrow, that spot feels a little fuzzy, and it feels like my top and bottom eyelashes are magnets trying to snap together. And also one of my eyelids keeps twitching.

I give my head a quick shake. This is no time for twitching!

I slide back a little on the seat as the bus turns up the tree-lined driveway to school. I look out, pressing my forehead to the rattly window to see if I can spot my friends up in the courtyard. The cold glass feels good on my head, and the vibrations of the bus feel kind of soothing. The heat is blasting, the bus is gently rocking. My eyelids droop. I take an extended blink.

"Hey. Kid. We're here."

I make a sound like *"Muh?"* and pull my face away from the glass, leaving a cold, flat feeling on my forehead. I stand up quickly, fumbling to adjust my backpack, which must have slipped down my shoulders when I dozed off. The bus driver watches me in the long rearview mirror as I hurry down the aisle, mumble "Thanks," and join the throng of kids soaking their sneakers in the still-wet leaves brought to the ground by yesterday's storm.

My five-minute bus nap has left me feeling all discombobulated and sleepier than I was before. Now I'm kind of unsure about my plan of just marching up to where my friends are clustered together on a damp bench and somehow popping the bubble of forgetfulness that has made them erase me from their memories.

I get this pull of yearning, seeing how complete they look, sitting so closely that their corduroy knees touch, the hoods of their stripy sweatshirts pulled up over their heads against the morning chill, their coordinated backpacks propped against the colorful laces of their high-tops. Do they feel my absence at all? Like a phantom limb?

I gulp, and weave my way through the crowd until I'm standing right in front of them.

". . . it awful? You can tell me the truth," Piper is saying with comic anxiousness. She has her sweatshirt unzipped barely an inch, exposing a pie-shaped sliver of her T-shirt, which is glaringly bright with wide, neon yellow and red stripes. I've never seen the shirt before, so I'm guessing Ms. Packenbush has pulled down another bag of her older daughters' used clothes from the attic.

"Whoa," Fee says, pointedly putting on her sunglasses, "turn the volume down on that thing."

All Celeste can do is wince and say, "Well, it's . . . colorful?"

"I knew it!" Piper wails, yanking the zipper back up and laying her head on Celeste's shoulder and groaning. "I look like the Undead Hot Dog Ladies Man!" My heart lurches a little; I know *just* which hot dog man Piper's talking about because I was there with them at Hampton Beach when we saw him at the end of summer. I'd managed to get a sunburn on one butt cheek, and Celeste had a stomachache from eating a piece of fried dough as big as her head, and Fee had a between-the-toes blister from her fancy new flip-flops, and Piper was freaking out because we were going to be late to meet her mom, and we rushed past this hot dog cart manned by a guy who looked like he was just dug up from a grave. He saw us running by and called out, "Hot dog, ladies?" We laughed so hard that we forgot all about sunburns, blisters, and bellyaches. At least, the bellyache was forgotten until Celeste ralphed in the car.

"I like it," I rush out. It comes out a croak.

"Excuse me?" Fee says as all three look up at me.

I clear my throat, slip my hands into the pockets of my own stripy sweatshirt. "I said I like your shirt." I look at Piper. "A lot of kids were wearing them in Brooklyn."

"You're from Brooklyn?" Fee asks, lifting her sunglasses. "That's SO cool."

I shrug like *Yeah, I know. No biggie.*

"Hey, you called me last night, right?" Piper asks, a smile playing at one side of her mouth. "That was kind of weird."

"Oh, yeah," Fee says, "you're the new kid working with Zooey in social studies, right?"

"I guess. Yes, but . . ." I falter, wondering if this is what I'll have to do: Start our friendship over from scratch?

"Just so you know," Fee says conspiratorially, "that girl is kind of persona non grata right now."

"Fee!" Celeste says in shock. "Don't spread that bad mojo."

"What?" Fee asks hotly. "The new kid should know what she's getting into."

"Anyway!" I look around. There are still a ton of kids in the courtyard, and if my plan fails, I don't want anybody to see it. "Can I sit down?"

"Oh, sure," Piper says, nudging Fee over to make room for me. "Make sure you sit just on the edge; the bench is kind of wet."

"My mom goes to New York City all the time for business," Celeste offers. "I got to stay with her once. They put us up at the Mandarin."

"Must be weird, moving here from Brooklyn. What was it like there?" Fee asks.

"It was fine," I say quickly as I sit down. Fee looks disappointed. "The thing is," I say, looking each of them in the eye, "we actually *didn't* meet just yesterday."

"What do you mean?" Fee asks. "You've, like, visited before or something?"

"Not exactly." I lower my voice. "We've actually been best friends since summer."

"Ooookay," Piper says, chuckling uncomfortably.

"We were best friends, but over this weekend, at the Harvest Festival"—I pause, they lean closer, curious—"I was jinxed. And you guys forgot me."

I watch Piper anxiously for her reaction. Her eyes widen for barely a second with something like recognition, and I feel this cool wash of relief start to spill over me, but then . . . she blinks. And then blinks again, and her brow

94

gets all wrinkly. She gives her head a sharp shake and then reels back a little as she looks at me.

"Do . . . do we know you?" she asks, as if she just noticed me sitting next to her.

"Yeah, are you new here?" Celeste asks, ticking her head to the side and looking at me like she's trying to place where she's seen me before.

"Wait, what?" I ask, the feeling of relief quickly morphing into cold dread.

"If it *is* your first day," Fee says as she and the others stand up, "you should get inside before the late bell."

They leave me sitting alone in the courtyard, Celeste holding one of the glass doors behind her for a second, before looking back to see that I'm still on the bench. She shrugs and goes inside.

"What just happened?" I whisper to the wind, shivering as it answers with a gust that sends fallen leaves skittering across the cobblestones.

They forgot me. Again. But it seemed different this time. More permanent. Was it because I told them about the jinx? Did I somehow make it worse?

My stomach lurches as I have a terrible thought: What if EVERYONE has forgotten me now? I yank my phone out of the front pocket of my backpack, because if this isn't a reason to break the no-phones-during-school-hours rule, I don't know what is!

"Dentist's office."

"Lucia! Is my dad there?"

"He's with a patient, Hattie," she says, her voice concerned. "Everything okay?"

I let out a small breath of relief when she says my name. "Fine. Can you just . . . tell him I'm on the phone?"

A moment later, the familiar high, gravelly tone of my dad's voice almost sends me into tears. "Hattie Cakes? Everything okay?"

I swallow back relieved tears. "Fine! I just . . . I wanted to tell you that, um"—my mind spins, trying to think of something—"I have to . . . um . . . stay after school today."

"Oh, okay," he says. "Field hockey, right? I have late hours tonight, so just come by the office when you're done with practice."

When I hang up, I take a deep breath and let it out slowly. It comes out as a shudder. So at least my dad and Lucia remember me. But what if it's just grown-ups who do? What if no kid in the entire world remembers me?

I look frantically around the empty courtyard and am about to bolt for the front doors of school to accost the first kid I see, when I notice a sleek black car idling at the curb. The passenger-side door opens, and out steps none other than Zooey Dutchman Zervos.

"*GAH!*" she cries as I interrupt her scan of the courtyard by jumping in front of her and demanding, "Do you know me?"

She somehow manages to scowl down at me, even though I'm taller than her. "Maybe?" she says, shrugging and walking past me.

"What's my name, then?" I ask, locking step with her as we walk across the wet cobblestone courtyard.

She huffs impatiently at me. "I don't know. Marcia or something?"

"Marcia?" I cry, stopping cold. It's so far off from my real, actual name that it doesn't even sound like a name at all, which somehow makes the fact that she doesn't know me even worse. "This can't be happening," I whisper, a sense of surrealness crashing over me.

"Look," she says over her shoulder, sounding annoyed as she yanks open one of the glass front doors to school. "Are we going to meet up about our project or what?"

"You DO remember!" I practically yell, pushing after her through the door.

As soon as the warm inside air of the towering atrium hits my chilled skin, my nose starts streaming and my glasses fog up, rendering me pretty much useless for the minute it takes me to find a balled-up tissue in my sweatshirt pocket, wipe my nose, and then, realizing I don't want to wipe my glasses with a booger cloth, lift the hem of my

T-shirt to wipe the condensation off my glasses. When I slide them back onto the bridge of my nose, Zooey comes into focus. Standing there smirking at me.

"You done?" she asks.

I raise my chin. "Yes. Quite."

"This project is like a third of our grade," Zooey says seriously. She unzips her coat. "Of course I remember my partner."

"But you don't remember my name," I remind her as we start across the linoleum tile inlay of Joseph Trepan's silhouette, which stretches across the whole floor of the atrium.

She sighs again, a chunky sound. "You're Hattie."

"Wait. You DO remember me!" I practically shriek.

She recoils, the same motion she made the second day of school when Piper asked if she could borrow a pencil. "Calm yourself," she says.

"But you remember who I am?" I ask firmly, ignoring her tone.

She shrugs. "I guess."

"You were just messing with me to be mean?" I ask. "What kind of person are you?!"

Going toe-to-ballet-flat with Zooey Dutchman Zervos is *not* on my list of things to do today, but today has gone so wackady-wackadoodle already that it's like all normal rules of self-preservation are off. This can't be my real life. This can't really be happening right now. I can't really be standing here glaring at Zooey, the person who Piper says can sense both fear and whether or not a girl has gotten her period.

Zooey kind of smirks and shrugs. But then she winces, and then she sighs.

I raise my eyebrows. "Are you okay?" I ask.

"I am sorry," she says, enunciating.

"Okay," I say, enunciating back.

Something in her face changes when she flicks her eyes up over my head for a split second. I turn and look behind me at the sleek wall of windows that line the front office. Sitting next to each other in the waiting area, throwing Zooey some major hairy eyeball, are Teagan and Tess.

The heat of their gaze shooting past me makes me snap my eyes down at my shoes, and I pretend to be really interested in the fact that I am standing right on the pointy chin of the Joseph Trepan silhouette outlined in the rubbery linoleum tile. I sneak a glance back up through the glass. They're still looking, a synchronized snarl aimed right at Zooey's face. I look at her to see if maybe she's crying or bursting into flames or something, but she's just smirking back at them like it doesn't even affect her, which is pretty amazing because I feel singed just from the secondhand heat.

Finally, Zooey starts walking toward the sixth-grade locker hall. "Meet me after school so we can get started on the project."

"Today?" I ask, hurrying after her. "I can't today."

She doesn't slow her stride. "Why not?"

"Because I said so!" I snap, since telling her the truth is not an option. I'm guessing that telling even *one more* person about the jinx would send the whole world into insta-amnesia.

Zooey slows just a bit so she can look at me. In fact, she looks at me like she's never seen me before, and I am suddenly about to barf from fear that *she's* suddenly forgotten me, too. "You're a weird one, aren't you?" she asks.

"Seriously?" I say, almost laughing from shock. "Who just calls people names to their faces?!"

Zooey makes a frustrated sound in her throat. "Sorry!" she says. "This is why I try not to speak!" She takes a deep breath and then says firmly, "You'll meet me. Unless you want us to fail." She comes to a complete stop and glares at me. "And failure is not an option."

She stalks away, her ballet flats making soft *scuff scuff scuff* sounds across Joseph Trepan's giant chin.

"You're not the boss of me!" I call after her, and though my voice barely makes it out of my mouth, she gives me a very rude gesture in response from the other end of the hall.

* * *

I've never been to the nurse's office at my new school because I kind of assumed it would be the same as the one at my school in Brooklyn: a cramped room that smells like old Band-Aids with no place to lie down.

But there is no way I can just waltz into first period and act like this whole day isn't one hundred percent CRAZY! I need to, like . . . meditate or center myself or something for, like, half a minute, until I can get my bearings and figure out what to do.

So ten minutes later, I've made my way down the back corridor of the school to the nurse's office; I am lying on a cot in a dimly lit room, covered by a soft white blanket, the comforting weight of a hot water bottle on my belly. Fibbing is not my strong suit, so instead of saying I *had* cramps, I said I thought that I might be about to get a cramp. Which is true. Because cramps are definitely in my near future, according to both the library and my mother, who, combined, know everything there is to know about puberty.

Meditate, Hattie, I tell myself. *CALM YOURSELF DOWN!*

Is shouting at yourself inside your own brain part of meditation?

I wish Celeste were here. She could tell me. Celeste is

101

excellent at meditation. She says it's her secret weapon to keep from barfing before competitions. Once, before a math test, I was sort of stuck in the hallway, so nervous that it felt like I couldn't physically make myself walk through the door. Celeste took one look at me and said, *Give those here.* She took my books and told me to close my eyes. She told me to take a deep breath. *Belly breaths,* she said, and then I felt her palm press gently against my belly button. *Fill up your belly.* I did what she said a few times, until I felt her hand drop away. I opened my eyes, blinking, and she gave me a small smile, handed me my books, and walked into class. Right then is when it dawned on me that Celeste and I almost never hang out, just the two of us. And I wondered why that was.

This time it takes me only seventeen seconds of belly breaths to send me straight to dreamland, and it feels like eighteen seconds before the nurse wakes me up again. Apparently, I've slept through first period and didn't meditate and still don't have my bearings and still have no idea what I'm going to do. As the nurse empties the water bottle into the sink and waits for me to tie my high-tops, I take quick stock of my situation.

The bad news:

I've been jinxed.

The *really* bad news:

The jinx is getting worse.

The *really, really* bad news:

I don't know how to break it.

The good news:

It's only my friends who've forgotten me. Everyone else seems to remember.

The *really* good news:

. . .

That one stumps me, until I realize there *has* to be a way to break the jinx. I mean, some official way, like jumping in a circle three times while holding my breath.

"You must be feeling better," the nurse says, watching me with a confused look. I just nod in response until I finish jumping my last rotation, let my breath out in a gush, and then stand totally still. Do I feel any different? Not a bit. I didn't think that would work. I mean, not really.

"I'm fine, thanks," I grumble. I need answers, and with a little excited gasp, I realize just where to find them. "I'm going to the library!"

"You need to go to social studies first!" she calls after me.

chapter Eleven

She's right. I do have to go to social studies first.

And I have to get through it with my friends barely even looking in my direction.

By the time I ask Mr. Zubki if I can spend another lunch at the library, I am so anxious to find information, so sure that it is waiting for me right on the tip of the Internet's tongue, that I feel like I'm going to jump out of my skin if I don't find it *right now*.

I slide action-movie-star style into the chair in the same computer carrel I used yesterday, shaking the mouse to wake up the computer monitor and then typing as fast as I can: "How to break a Harvest Jinx, Trepan's Grove." And then I type it again, more slowly this time, because the first time I actually typed "alksamcwoeaitfhasdlkfd."

I hold my breath as the results come up. My eyes focus on the bold phrases highlighted in each result, all the way down the page, each a variation of:

There is no way to break a Harvest Jinx.

"No way?" I whisper, clicking to the next page of results and seeing the same thing. "No way!" I go through six pages of results before I finally face the truth.

According to the Internet, there is no way to break a Harvest Jinx.

Mr. Zubki isn't much more help. Apparently, accosting the librarian and begging to see the history section is not something people do in Trepan's Grove on any sort of regular basis. He seems a bit taken aback by the fact that he has to peel my white-knuckled fingers off his suspenders.

He keeps his distance and gestures toward the small local history section of our school library, but the books have only passing mention of Trepan's Grove, and none mentions the jinx.

"Maybe try the town library?" he suggests.

"You're a genius!" I whisper-yell, my hands reaching for his suspenders. Mr. Zubki takes a step back.

Of course the town library will have information on the jinx! They probably have a book called simply *The Jinx* that they keep in a glass cabinet with its own spotlight.

You know what they don't have at the town library? A book called *The Jinx* kept in a glass cabinet with its own spotlight. They don't even have a book called *The Jinx* that they use as a doorstop. They don't have any books about the jinx at all. Well, that's not totally true. The librarian, who has no suspenders for me to grab on to, leads me upstairs to what she calls the mezzanine. It's a kind of balcony looking over the main floor of the library, and it's where the history books are kept.

It's also where you can spy on the friends who have forgotten you because you accidentally jinxed yourself.

Celeste and Fee are sitting with their heads close together at one of the giant, dark wood tables on the first floor, and I can tell by the way they are moving in sync that they are sharing a pair of earbuds. I watch as they both lean back, press one hand to their hearts, point to each other with their free hand, and lip-sync what I'm sure is a rap song. I suck in my lips to keep from laughing as I watch them trade whispered rap verses and then silently groove back into the chorus. The song ends and they pop out their earbuds, then pull out the assignment sheet for social studies.

Social studies.

Oh, *shoot*!

I actually ditched Zooey Dutchman Zervos.

I'd left school through the back exit, wanting to avoid everybody. I wonder if she's still waiting for me out front. I bet I could walk back up to school and find her. Or . . . I could just stay here, leaning against the end of a bookcase behind the railing, out of sight of everyone on the first floor. Celeste and Fee are discussing the project now, and both are laughing and getting shushed by the librarian.

I remember maybe a week or so after Celeste got back from skating camp, we were all supposed to meet at the Chin on the common and then walk down to the town pond. This was right before I sprained my ankle. I was sitting on the porch rocker at the Dentist's House, my feet up on the balcony, rereading Tilde's Realm #2 and keeping an eye on the common, watching out for when my friends started to show up. Celeste and Fee arrived at the same time, and I stuck my book under the cushion of the rocker, knocked on the window frame, called good-bye to my dad inside the office, and trotted across the street. Fee and Celeste were walking arm in arm toward the Chin, and what I did felt so natural and so right that I didn't even think about it. Or maybe I did. Maybe I thought, *This is what Piper would do!* I ran up and sort of nudged between them, linking elbows with them and grinning like *Surprise!* And Fee laughed and said, "Brooklyn!" but Celeste reeled back, almost dropping my arm. If Piper hadn't run up to us at that exact moment, I think Celeste would have said something. But she snapped out of it, smiled, and was perfectly friendly. Though she just felt . . . closed. Yes, *closed* is the right word.

When Piper plops down in a chair across from Fee and Celeste, I seriously almost cry out. I want to scream, *"I'M*

HERE!" and I want them to call my name again and again until I limp right into their arms.

But I don't say anything. And neither do they.

I just sit and watch as Fee and Celeste work on their project, and Piper does her own homework. An hour goes by and the sun dips into the high windows across from the balcony, so orange and bright that I have to get up to keep from being blinded. I should be getting to the Dentist's House anyway. Dad will be expecting me.

Shoot, I say to myself when I get outside and see Fee getting into her mom's shiny red pickup. She doesn't notice me, which gives me a chance to hear the first part of her conversation with her mom:

"How did that go?"

"What do you mean? It went fine."

"Was that Piper there, too?"

I can hear Fee's sigh all the way up the walkway, where I stand by the front door. "Yeah, but she's not in our group. She's not on the project."

"Well, that's good," Mrs. Goody says, in a not entirely nice way. "And what about Teagan and Tess?"

Fee doesn't say anything.

"Fiona? Have you talked to them at least?"

Fee sighs again. "Not really."

"Well, I'm going to call their moms. Just to check in."

What in the world is that all about?

chapter
twelve

Wednesday is pretty much like Tuesday, except I write a different date on the top of my notes before totally zoning out in every class, trying to think my way out of the jinx. I avoid Zooey's gaze for all of social studies and wait a full thirty minutes before heading out of school at the end of the day, but there she is: waiting for me on one of the large decorative boulders that mark the entrance to the courtyard.

"Oh, heck no," I grumble as soon as I see her. Zooey turns at the sound of my voice and slides off the rock, slinging her backpack over her shoulder. I could run back inside the school, but she's standing between me and the path to the library.

"You ditched me," she says, sounding annoyed and a little impressed, once I'm directly in front of her.

"Look," I say, sighing, "I told you I couldn't work on our project yesterday. And I can't today, either. I have to get home."

She gives me a funny look and says sarcastically, "Don't be too excited about working together or anything."

"Trust me, I'm not," I reply testily.

Zooey doesn't even extend the energy to make a full eye roll. She just flicks her eyes up and to the left. "Obviously."

"Sorry if you thought I was going to, like, fawn all over you," I blurt out, a sickly shiver washing over me at the unfamiliar feeling of being mean to someone's face. Is this how Zooey feels all the time? "I'm not one of your followers."

"I don't *have* followers," she says sharply.

"Not anymore," I respond icily.

Then I wince. Because Zooey winced. And I realize that I would make a terrible popular mean girl because I would just be hugging people ALL THE TIME, because how can you not after saying something that makes someone look the way Zooey looks right now?

"Sorry," I mumble. And then I wonder, who has Zooey been hanging out with since she was defriended? I mean, that was last week, like, a whole lifetime ago. "So . . ." I falter. "Who are you, like, hanging out with now?"

"None of your business. Who do you hang out with?" she shoots back.

I blink at her, her question bringing up an answer to a question I hadn't even thought of asking, and my attention goes from the hurt feelings of Trepan's Grove former Teen Queen to my own surreal set of circumstances. "Do *you* know who I hang out with?"

Her top lip goes all squirmy. "You are *so* weird."

"No, really," I say, suddenly desperate. "Do you know who my friends are?"

She lets out a huff of air. "Do you? I think that's the real question."

I just blink at her.

"Fine," she says. "No, I don't know who your real friends are. Happy?"

"Not at all," I say, my voice small. I take a deep breath and add this new tidbit of information to my list. *Nobody else remembers my friendships either.*

Zooey sighs again. "So . . . can we go now?"

I blink at her. "You still . . . you still want to be my partner? I mean, we were just, like, *really* mean to each other. I, for one, am still smarting. I think . . ." I pause, pretending to think. "I think maybe we should just go our separate ways and ask Ms. Lyle if we can do independent projects instead."

Zooey does the thing I've gotten used to since our first conversation yesterday: She watches me through half-shut eyes, like she's trying to bring me into focus.

"No," she says. "That doesn't work for me. We have to turn in the topic of our paper on November first. That's in two weeks. We have to start now. And we'll get docked if we don't work together."

"Fine."

We walk out of the courtyard and start down the sidewalk, our feet shuffling through the fallen leaves, which have dried out a bit since yesterday. Out of the corner of my eye, I can see she's looking at me. "Are you about to cry?" she asks, a little accusingly.

"No!" I answer, giving my face a good rub. "I'm just allergic to nature."

From our right comes another voice. "Hattie!" I look over to see Ms. Thackary, our gym teacher and field hockey coach, sailing over the stone wall that borders the practice field. She manages to jog easily up the steep slope to the sidewalk.

"Oh, great," I groan. I can't believe I forgot about practice again. Zooey takes this opportunity to step away and text.

"I'm so sorry I missed practice," I say before she's even in front of us. She's barely panting at all!

"What do you mean?" she asks. "Practice for what?"

A shivery feeling crawls up my back. "Field hockey?" I answer as a question.

"We're full into the season," she says brightly. "If you want to play next year, sign up! But I hope to see you at basketball tryouts next week." She gives my height an up-and-down glance. "We could really use someone like you." She smiles and nods at Zooey, and then jogs back down the hill, leaping over the stone wall as she calls out the next drill for the team.

"Holy cannoli," I whisper. Did that just really happen? Did she really forget I was ever on the team? If she did, why didn't she forget me, too? Then I remember. The day of field hockey sign-ups, Piper was the one who wrote down my name on the paper Ms. Thackary hung up outside the gym. This just keeps getting weirder and weirder.

"So let's get to the library," I say as Zooey and I start walking again.

"Not the library," she says firmly.

"But that's where all the books are!" I say. Then I follow her gaze down the sidewalk, where the last kids from school, including the Ts, are turning toward town, most likely heading for the library to work on their own projects.

"All the books and all the jerks," she answers, ignoring my surprised look at the fact that she's actually acknowledging what happened last week in the cafeteria. "Let's go to the historical society instead."

A lightbulb goes off in my head.

"Wait. They have books about Trepan's Grove there, right?" I ask. I start to walk faster.

"Uh. *Yeah*. It's the Trepan's Grove Historical Society."

"So they'd have books about the jinx, right?"

"The Harvest Jinx? Yeah, I guess. Why?"

"*That's* what we should do our project on!" I say, realizing that if I can convince Zooey of this, she can help me find a way to break the jinx.

"The jinx?" Zooey scoffs, leading us under the blinking yellow traffic light that hangs over Main Street, and into the parking lot in front of the Trading Post. "Why? It's just a dumb kids' poem. I thought we could do it on women's rights in Colonial times."

I hesitate. That actually sounds really interesting. I glance up at the glassed-in porch of the Trading Post. "Oh, are we getting candy first? I could actually use a grape Fizzy Fuzz." My mouth waters at the thought.

Zooey shakes her head at me and points hard at the small painted HISTORICAL SOCIETY sign hanging by the door of the Trading Post. I'd never noticed it before.

"I have to call my mom," she says. "I'll meet you upstairs."

"Great! I'll get started!" I say, yanking open the screen door and hurrying through the porch and into the Trading Post. I do a quick scan of the place and wonder how it is I never saw the hand-painted wooden sign next to a door on the back wall, reading TREPAN'S GROVE HISTORICAL SOCIETY. ATTIC.

chapter thirteen

The staircase is narrow and dusty and dark, and for a second, I wish Zooey was with me, but I push myself to go all the way up on my own.

Whoa.

It is basically one huge room covering the whole span of the Trading Post. The roof starts just a few feet from the floor, slants up on both sides, peaking high overhead. And the place is packed. Not in a messy way, but in an every-square-inch-is-being-used way. Rows and rows of heavy wooden bookshelves cram the floor, the taller ones in the middle and shorter ones along the edges where the roof stretches down. Framed photographs and paintings of all different sizes are mounted haphazardly to the wood paneling, reaching almost all the way to the high peak of the roof.

A long, faded rug runs the width of the attic between rows of shelves, from the top of the stairs to a huge, old-fashioned green metal desk at the back.

"Hello?" I call, and when no one answers, I start to scan the list of titles on the bookshelf closest to the stairs. With an excited gasp, I pull out a short and slim volume called *Trepan's Grove Traditions*. It's a hardcover book with a clear, crinkly library cover over the yellowing white dust jacket. I flip it open and see it's old but not super old, written in 1988.

"Done and done!" I whisper excitedly. I'll have the jinx broken by sundown.

The book opens, as I'd expect it to, with the poem.

Make a promise before you think, and you could get a Harvest Jinx!

Fall Harvest Festival visitors to the picturesque town of Trepan's Grove, Massachusetts, will hear a lot about the Harvest Jinx, the folksy town legend that warns all who make a promise on Harvest to keep a promise on Harvest, whether you want to or not.

I'm so entranced by what I'm reading that I don't notice someone approach me, until a hot breath ruffles the short hair at the nape of my neck.

"Ahhh!" I jump around and raise my hands in karate-chop formation.

And much to my surprise, it's Maude smirking back at me. "I startled you. How exciting."

I blink at her, my voice caught in my throat.

"What've you got there?" she asks, folding her arms over her chest.

"Nothing?" I answer, quickly hiding the book behind my back.

She eyes me through a pair of perfectly round plastic-framed glasses in bright yellow. They clash spectacularly with the purple full-body jumpsuit she has on. She nods toward my arm, the one holding the book from sight. "That's town property, you know. Don't make me apprehend you."

"I wasn't . . . I'm not . . ." I falter. "It's for a project." I hold the book out to her. She takes it, the fabric of her jumpsuit crinkling as she does.

"Hm. The jinx," she says, glancing at the cover of the book and then back up at me. "Aren't you a little old for this sort of thing? We covered it in second grade."

"I didn't grow up here," I answer, turning as I hear Zooey trudging up the stairs. She pauses for a moment at the top, taking it all in. Then she sees Maude and me and raises an eyebrow.

"Hello," Maude says to her, flatly, as she approaches.

"Hey, didn't you used to be that kid genius who goes to MIT?" Zooey asks.

I look in confusion at Maude. This Fizzy Fuzz thief is a genius?

117

Maude answers quickly, "I'm eighteen. Not a kid. And I don't go to MIT. Who says I go to MIT?"

"*Um* . . . everyone," Zooey says.

"I *went* to MIT. Now I *teach* at MIT," Maude says. "Or at least I used to. I'm on sabbatical. *Voluntary.* Sabbatical."

"Why?" Zooey asks.

"Familial obligations and nostalgia for childhood."

"I thought childhood was a wound," I counter.

Maude gives me an almost pleased look. "I did say that, didn't I? I guess I'm back to examine the scars."

I make a strange sound in my throat, no idea how to respond. Maude lets out a sigh and gives me a pitying look. She finally says, "Oh, don't get so freaked out. Look, my mom usually manages this place, but she hurt her back and asked me to come home and take over for the fall semester. So here I am. But the scar stuff . . ." she adds quickly. "That's all true, too. I ran out of here like a bat out of heck when I was twelve, and never looked back. I kind of wonder if that did something to me. You know . . . emotionally. Anyway. What do you want?"

Zooey says, "We want to do a project for social studies."

"On the Harvest Jinx . . ." I chime in.

"Boring," Maude says dismissively. "Choose something else and *maybe* I'll help you."

"That's what I told her," Zooey says, scanning the packed space. "The jinx is kid stuff."

"It's not, though!" I say quickly, sounding just like a kid. "I mean, we all know the poem, but no one knows when it was written—"

"In 1956," Maude responds.

I glare at her and continue, "Or *why* it was written."

"To celebrate our town's bicentennial."

I huff at her. "Or why it doesn't include anything about how to break the jinx."

"You can't break a Harvest Jinx," Maude and Zooey say at the same time.

"Besides," Zooey informs me, "it's made up. You can't break something that's made up."

I make a sound in my throat like a toad being smooshed mid-croak.

Zooey wrinkles her nose at the sound and then says, "Anyway. I don't remember anything about how to break it, just like the rules and stuff."

"Rules?" I squeak. "There are RULES?!"

"Yeah, like, don't tell anybody if you get jinxed or you make it worse. That kind of thing." Zooey looks at Maude. "Right?"

"Hold everything!" I practically shout, waving my hands like I'm shooing away bees. "You make it worse if you tell someone?"

Zooey and Maude give me almost identical, incredulous looks, and say, "Uh, *yeah*?" at the same time.

"Why do you care so much?" Maude adds sharply.

"Because . . . because . . . I . . . think that's important information! You know, for our project? Accuracy! And . . . um . . . inclusion of the factual facts about the things!" They do not look impressed. "This project is a third of our grade," I say, trying not to sound as desperate as I feel. "It's important we get it right." I try to act nonchalant, like this isn't a matter of life and death. To do this, I lean *very casually* against a bookshelf. "So. Are there other rules?"

Maude reaches out and lays her fingertips on my shoulders and firmly shifts me into an upright position. Then she says, "I don't remember. They're in the poem."

"The 'Make a Promise' poem?" I ask, trying to remember any mention of rules in what Piper said.

"Well, the long version," Maude says.

"A long version? Is it in the book?" I reach for it. Maude pulls it away.

"This book?" She looks at it like she's not impressed. "Not likely."

"Where can I find it, then?"

Maude snorts. "Good luck. It was probably typed out for the bicentennial and then lost in the back of someone's junk drawer."

"It could be around here somewhere, though, right?" I ask, scanning the crowded room. "We could use it for our project."

"Maybe," Maude says, but she doesn't sound convinced. "I don't think it was ever published."

"Wait, wait, wait," Zooey says. "I never agreed to do our project on the jinx. I want to do it on women in Colonial times."

I look at Zooey. I mean really look at her. Sure, she has popular-girl eye power, but I have the eye power of the jinxed. And I will not be denied. "Imagine, if you will," I say gravely, "we were able to find the 'Lost Poem of Trepan's Grove.'"

"No one actually calls it that," Maude mutters beside me.

I ignore her. "We'd be hailed as heroes."

"Doubtful," Maude says.

Zooey snorts, but then says, "Look, you see what you can find about the jinx, and maybe we can include it. But that's not enough for a whole ten-page paper."

"Can you just help us find the Harvest Jinx poem?" I ask Maude impatiently. "Kind of on a schedule here."

Maude turns to Zooey and does a quick no-look side nod in my direction. "Your friend's a little intense."

"She's not my friend," Zooey corrects her quickly.

"Well, *she's* not anybody's friend," I tell Maude, hating how bratty my voice sounds.

"Ah, you're that girl who was defriended?" Maude says, ignoring the horrible thing I just said and nodding at Zooey.

Zooey looks a little sick. "You heard about that?"

"Your nonfriend told me," Maude answers. Another side nod in my direction.

Zooey narrows her eyes and shakes her head at me. She seems more upset about the fact that I told Maude than the fact that I said she has no friends.

"Sorrynotsorry," I say, jutting out my chin. Even though I am actually a little sorry. Maybe Zooey was hoping there was at least one person in Trepan's Grove who hadn't heard about what happened to her. "Can we just start researching now?"

"Yes," Zooey says acidly. "Let's get this over with."

"This way," Maude says, stepping sideways and out of sight between two bookcases.

"Go ahead," Zooey says, waiting for me to follow Maude. I do, slipping my backpack off and carrying it so it won't knock books off the shelf. My eyes scan the shelves as we pass, hundreds and hundreds of books, with titles like *New England History 1700–1820*, all carefully encased in the smooth, clear plastic protective covers that make that wonderful crinkly sound when I brush by. I can't move my arm up, so I let my fingers run over the spines behind me as I pass. The books smell old, wonderfully old, and even though the old scent makes my nose start to run, I inhale deeply.

"Will you hurry up?" Zooey growls behind me.

"I am," I say, looking ahead to see Maude waiting for us where the bookshelves end.

She's led us to a little nook in front of the dormer window that looks over Main Street and the common beyond.

Maude pulls the cord on a wooden floor lamp with a tasseled shade. A threadbare but colorful rug is laid out in the narrow space, along with a few giant embroidered throw pillows propped up against one of the whitewashed dormer walls.

"It's like your own little . . . nook."

"It's the town's nook," Maude corrects me. "These are the books specifically about Trepan's Grove history. Zooey, if you want to focus on women's roles in town, you can use all of these books. Hattie, the jinx wasn't made up until two hundred years later, so look for books published after 1956."

And then, like a ghost, she steps back between the bookshelves and disappears, the sound of her crinkling jumpsuit fading as she does, leaving Zooey and me in the silent little nook.

Charming Traditions of Small Town New England. This could have something on the jinx.

Zooey sits as far away from me as she can in the confines of the nook, takes a book off the top of a pile, and opens it. "Hey," she says, "why'd—"

I hold up a finger to get her to stop talking while I scan the chapter called "Seasonal Festivals," and Zooey makes an annoyed sound in her throat. "Dang it," I say, dropping my finger and putting the book back on top of the stack. "This doesn't really have anything about the jinx." I grab the next book from the stack and start flipping through the pages.

"Why'd you tell Maude about what happened to me?" Zooey asks.

I look up from the book. "I don't know," I answer honestly. "It just kind of popped out the other day."

"Yeah, well, if you don't mind, I don't need you gossiping about me with the town genius."

"About that . . ." I whisper, lowering the book and glancing toward the aisle to make sure Maude isn't there. "She's really a genius?"

She scoffs. "You've never heard of Maude Faem?"

"No, I've never heard of Maude Faem. I didn't grow up here, remember?"

"Yeah, that's obvious," Zooey says. "Look, Maude's a genius. She was in my older brother's grade, with the Packenbush twins, but left Trepan's Grove when she was twelve to go to college early. She's been gone ever since. And she's apparently turned into some kind of weirdo."

"Seriously, what have you got against weirdos?" I ask hotly.

Zooey shrugs. Clears her throat. Takes a deep breath. And then says, "Nothing. Sorry. But just for your information, I *have* friends. They're just not at this school."

"Got it," I say.

"Good," she answers. Then she picks up a book and opens it, and doesn't look up at me again.

I tell myself it's fine that I can see tears welling up in her eyes and that she turns a page loudly to cover the sound of a sniff. Zooey Dutchman Zervos has never been nice to me, I tell myself. She's never been *anything* to me. And she's been really mean to my friends. She wipes her eyes with her wrist.

I pick up my own book and start to scan.

I fall into the research, feeling more and more disheartened as I flip through volume after volume that mentions only the first line of the Harvest Jinx poem.

"My mom's here," Zooey announces a long time later, startling me. She's standing up, stretching her long arms up over her head, her silver bangles sliding down to her elbows. "I found a bunch of stuff we can use on women in colonial times. You find anything?"

I shake my head. "Nothing." I pick up the dozen or so books I haven't gone through yet, slender volumes that feel too light in my hands, like there is no way they could hold what I'm looking for. I swallow down the lump in my throat. I really thought I would find the answer and things would be back to normal by tomorrow.

Zooey slides into her coat. "So we'll do our project on women in colonial times," she says firmly, as if her saying it makes it so. "We'll come back tomorrow and keep researching."

Maude's voice comes from somewhere beyond the bookshelves. "We're closed tomorrow. Open Tuesdays and Thursdays."

"But today's Wednesday, and you're open!" I object.

"I forgot to lock the door," Maude says. "And most people read the sign that says *Open Tuesdays and Thursdays* before barging in."

"So we'll come tomorrow," Zooey says. "It'll be Thursday."

"We'll be closed for a special event," Maude answers.

My heart sinks. "But I haven't found anything," I say, my voice sounding as hopeless as I feel.

Zooey tsks. "Well, we told you you wouldn't."

Maude slinks out from between the bookshelves. Her yellow glasses practically glow. She looks at the books in my hands. "This is a noncirculating library. You can't check books out. You have to come back Tuesday if you have more to do."

"Tuesday?" I ask weakly, looking at the books in my hands, flinching at the urge to take them the moment Maude's back is turned. I would never take them, not really. "That's next week."

"It's fine. There's stuff about women in colonial times in the library at school," Zooey says, zipping her coat and shrugging on her backpack. "I don't know if you're going to find anything else about the jinx," she says, "but we can come back here Tuesday if you want, and look again. I'll bring my laptop, and we can start writing up our topic proposal."

"Okay." My voice cracks again, and Zooey gives me a curious look.

"It's going to be okay, you know that, right?" she says, like it's obvious. "I'm a straight-A student." Maude makes a quiet scoffing noise at this. "And I've heard you answer questions in class. You're no dummy." Another scoff from Maude.

I make a choking half-laugh, half-sob sound. "Thanks?"

Maude studies me. "Are you okay? Technically speaking."

I look out the window into the darkness and blink back tears. "This has just been a long, weird, really stupidly stupid week," I answer, sniffing.

"Ditto," Zooey says. I turn to her, but she doesn't say anything more.

"I'll see what I can find out about the jinx before you come back next week," Maude says, her voice a little more gentle. I nod my thanks.

I still feel too much like crying to say anything, so I just replace the books I'm holding on their shelf, put on my jacket, and follow Zooey through the stacks and down the stairs.

chapter fourteen

I don't feel well," I moan the next morning, keeping my head buried in my pillow, not sure which parent has tip-toed into my room and opened my curtains, throwing a column of weak sunshine on my face.

A soft, cool hand on my forehead. *Oh, shoot*, I think, *it's Mom*. My plan of staying in bed every day until the historical society opens again on Tuesday is already in jeopardy. The problem with having a medical professional for a mother is that she has a very finely tuned Fake Sick detector. The mattress sinks a little as she sits down beside me on the bed.

"You're not warm," she murmurs, like she's talking to herself. "Here, sit up."

I do, as dramatically as I can without overacting. A smirk twitches just on the thick part of her lips. She presses her hand to the back of my neck, gives a small shake of her head. "Open," she says, and I do, stick out my tongue, and say, "Argggh."

"Hattie Cakes, you seem fine to me," Mom says. "Dad told me you conked out early last night. I think sleep is probably what you needed."

"I need more sleep," I say sleepily. "Sleep and your healing homemade bone broth."

Mom laughs, loud. "You hate soup."

"Only because it's soupy."

She looks at me for a moment. "Everything okay at school?"

I nod quickly. "Fine." *Apart from being jinxed and forced to work with Zooey.*

She looks at me for another long moment. "And your friends . . . ?" She blinks. "Your friends . . . What were their names?"

I blink back tears. I hadn't considered the possibility that my parents wouldn't remember my friends either. "I'm still sort of making friends, Mom." My voice comes out thick with emotion.

She pulls me into a hug. "It'll happen, hon," she says. "We just moved here a few months ago. It might take a little bit to find kids you really connect with." I rest my cheek on her shoulder and sigh. It's the same thing she said to me when we first moved here, right before I met Piper. I remember running up the steps and announcing,

"Connection: MADE!" She'd sort of quizzed me then: "Oh, does she love Tilde's Realm?" and "Has she seen that show you love, *Rosemary and Thyme*?" and finally, when I said no to both of those, "What's she think of cat T-shirts?"

"Mom," I had said, trying to hold on to my enthusiasm. "That was sort of Rae and Hattie stuff. It doesn't mean I can't have other stuff with other people." She had smiled, a little weakly, and said, "Okay. Glad you made a new friend."

And I was glad, too. But now everything was a mess.

"I really don't feel well," I tell my mom, pulling back.

She switches to her nurse voice. "Well, you have no fever. When was the last time you ate and what did you have?"

"Last night. Chili with Dad," I say cautiously, wondering where she's going with this information.

"I thought I smelled corn chips in the kitchen when I got home. When was the last time you moved your—"

"GETTING UP!" I yell, jumping out of bed before Mom can start asking me ultra-embarrassing questions about my bathroom habits.

She grins and walks to the bedroom door. "It's a miracle!" On her way downstairs, I hear her call to my dad, "SAL, SHE'S CURED!"

"She's so much less funny than she thinks she is," I tell Champ.

I take a pair of corduroys out of my dresser and then sit on my bed and scowl at them. The thought of another day spent *zip zip zipping* through the halls while being ignored by my friends exhausts me. I eye my dresser and then stretch my leg out from the bed. With my big toe I shimmy open the bottom drawer of my dresser, the one with the clothes I haven't worn since moving here from Brooklyn. I lean forward and peek in. A stack of neatly folded cat T-shirts. A colorful tangle of leggings.

"Look at you!" my dad says when I come downstairs. "You're like throwback Hattie!"

My mom ducks around the corner to see. "Brooklyn in the HOUSE!" she says loudly, in a completely mortifying voice. "Glad you're feeling better, kid."

I slump through breakfast—clumpy oatmeal my mom insists on, in case I actually am coming down with something. I hope for spontaneous barfing, but nothing happens. I'm going to have to go to school.

Mom and Dad team up to force me to wear an actual coat today, since it's the middle of October and getting colder by the minute. Of course, being a Girl Who Grows Taller on Days That End in *Y* means I grew out of my winter coat from last year and donated it before we left

Brooklyn. Mom goes to the hall closet and pulls out a coat that Uncle Joseph left the last time they were all here to watch a Red Sox game. "It was your cousin Gina's," Mom says. "It'll fit you perfectly."

"Cousin Gina we just checked into a nursing home?! Mom, that coat is, like, thirty years old!"

"No! Cousin Gina who just got married!"

"And it's L.L.BEAN!" my dad practically yells as he holds the coat out so I can slip my arms in. "This thing'll last forever!"

I begrudgingly shrug the coat on. It's red canvas on the outside with two giant pockets on the bottom, and I think it weighs more than our giant cat. The inside is a thick, plaid wool, and as soon as I get it on, my back starts to sweat.

"Get outside," my dad encourages me. "You'll melt with that thing on in here."

The bus driver echoes my dad's sentiment as I trudge up the steps. "You're going to roast."

I unzip it as I pass him.

"Nice coat, though," he calls after me down the aisle.

I shrug off the coat, pulling my cat T-shirt away from my back, letting the relatively chillier air cool my skin as I settle into a seat toward the back of the bus. I'm determined not to fall asleep again, and instead let the rumble of the bus send me into my memories.

The first time I met Piper was at the town beach.

She was wearing a sort of baggy blue swimsuit and sitting under a tree on a big blanket.

Over her swimsuit she was wearing a pair of cutoff jean shorts faded to a cloudy sky blue.

"Do you want to sit down?" she asked, moving a giant math workbook and three pencils to her other side and patting the now empty space on the blanket beside her. "It's kind of lumpy," she apologized as I sat. "You have to, like, find the perfect place for your butt between roots."

I moved a little, settled in, and laughed out loud. She was right!

"Told you!" Piper said brightly, stretching out her bare legs in front of her, and tapping the toes of her beat-up blue Converse together. She smoothed the Wonder Woman Band-Aid on her knee. "So are you just visiting, or do you live here?"

"Um, I live here now, I guess."

"Really?!" she asked excitedly, moving so she was sitting cross-legged. "Where are you from? Are you going into sixth? Where do you guys live?"

"Um . . . Brooklyn, yes, and Applewood Acres."

Her jaw dropped, her metal braces shining. "Really? My friend Fee is going to *flip* when she finds out you're from Brooklyn. She's, like, obsessed. Was it amazing? Fee says it's amazing, even though she's never been there. Celeste, she's our other best friend, she's been there with her mom, though. I've never been. But I have a sister who lives there! Her name's Periwinkle. She's a hairstylist. She did this . . ."

She acted like she was patting her hair—a cool-looking, short on the sides, swoop of bangs in the front, surfer-type do.

"I like it," I said.

"Thanks," she said. "So you live in . . . PEANUT!" She jumped and took two big steps toward the shore, where a little girl who looked to be about six was dragging a humongous fallen tree from the edge of the woods toward the water. She wore a Wonder Woman bathing suit and looked like a mini version of Piper.

"IT'S MY BOAT!" the little girl yelled, giving the tree another yank, and it carved a deep canyon in the sand as it moved, people dodging the clusters of branches as she went.

"Ugh, hold on," Piper grumbled, jogging down to the girl. I didn't hear the whole conversation, just that it involved mostly the words *no* and *Mom said* from Piper, and words like *canoe, not the boss of me, sailboat,* and *I just need an ax* from the little girl. I watched as Piper helped the girl drag the tree back to the woods, and they both walked back to the blanket, holding hands.

"I get a Popsicle," the girl informed me. "Pipey said."

"Sweet," I responded. The girl smiled at me and took the folded dollar bills Piper gave her from the beach bag.

"What kind do you want?" Piper asked.

"Oh! That's okay," I answered, even though a Popsicle would have been amazing right about then.

"It's no problem," Piper said. "Seriously, what's your favorite flavor?"

"Grape," I said, smiling. Peanut trotted off to the ice-cream truck, and Piper sat down, turning a little so she could keep an eye on Peanut.

"That's my little sister," Piper said with a grin. "She usurped me as the youngest Packenbush."

Here's what happened the rest of the afternoon: We ate Popsicles (Peanut snuck a bite of mine), we played a million games of Crazy Eights with Peanut, I helped Piper with her math, she told me about Celeste and Fee, and we helped Peanut make a tiny boat out of twigs and leaves and grass and nudged it out into the water, where it immediately sank and we all cracked up. I even tried swimming in the pond, even though I wouldn't go in above my waist. I'm used to swimming in pools, and you can't see the bottom of a pond. All those fish and slimy plants. Ick!

At the end of the day, we took turns giving Peanut piggyback rides through the center of town and up the hill to their house. I felt like I was glowing with happiness, and I practically floated back to the Dentist's House to tell my dad that I'd made a friend.

Does she like Tilde's Realm? I hear my mom asking, and even now I can feel my annoyance.

Warmed by the memory, I join the throng of kids passing through the courtyard into school when I get off the bus, zipping up my coat against the cold misting rain that is soaking everything. No one is hanging around outside. I step to the side when I'm through the front doors, taking a second to clean the fog off my glasses and wipe my nose with a tissue that is so old and linty, it may actually have ten-year-old Gina boogers on it.

"Nice coat!" I turn to see Belinda, the school secretary, leaning her puffy-haired head out of the office to holler at me and point with a sharp pink fingernail. "Classic Bean!"

"Uh, thanks?" I say awkwardly, avoiding the glances of my classmates, who don't look as impressed. Belinda ducks back into the front office and says something sharp to the Ts, who are once again sitting together, whispering, in their coordinated good-girl outfits, waiting to be brought into the suspension room. They roll their eyes in unison at Belinda's rebuke and slide over so there are two seats between them.

I hurry past, not wanting them to remember seeing me talk to Zooey and focus their laser beams on me.

I tune out the morning announcements as I make my way to my locker and shove Gina's coat in, having to use first my knee, then both elbows, and then my butt to get it all the way in before slamming my locker shut and growling, "Take that, you smarmy coat."

When I hear laughter, I look over and see Piper standing there. She's in a pair of jeans so faded and worn that there are patches where the threads are coming apart, giving a venetian-blind view of the rainbow stripes on the tights she wears underneath. On top she wears a seriously retro Trepan's Grove Appleseeds class sweatshirt that must have been one of her sister Periwinkle's. She laughs; her braces glint. "You are totally the boss of that coat!"

She looks so much like herself, I just grin back at her, because if I try to say anything, I might burst into tears.

"Are you new here?" she asks, stepping forward and holding out her hand for me to shake, confirming what I learned yesterday: She has forgotten me all over again. "I'm Piper Packenbush, of the Ladies Packenbush."

I shake her hand and swallow back the lump in my throat. "Hattie. And yeah. I'm new here."

"I have one of those, too," she says, nodding toward the red coat sleeve sticking out of my locker. "But mine's green. It was my sister's. It's going to last *forever.*"

"Mine was my cousin Gina's," I offer. "She's, like, thirty now."

She laughs a little, even though what I said wasn't that funny. I know that I'm looking at her in a sort of yearning way, and her eyes dart to the side uncomfortably. All I want to say is *You remember me, don't you, Pipes? Somewhere in there? You remember me, don't you?* But I don't say anything at all.

"Well, see ya," she says.

I nod. "See ya." And watch as she hurries down the hall to catch up with Fee and Celeste.

"You find anything?" I jump a little and turn to see Zooey leaning against the locker next to mine.

"Excuse me?" I say.

"About the jinx. Last night, online, after you got home from the historical society. You find anything?"

"Oh. No. I kind of passed out early . . ." I keep watching my three friends until they reach the end of the hall and turn. When I turn my attention back to Zooey, she lets out a huffy breath.

"Me either," she says sourly. "In case you were curious."

"You looked?" I ask, surprised. I thought she hated the idea of doing our project on the jinx.

She shrugged. "Your whole 'Lost Poem of Trepan's Grove' speech piqued my curiosity. Didn't find anything, though."

"You look tired." I say this before I can stop myself, and quickly follow it with "Sorry."

Zooey shrugs. "I am tired. I was up late."

"Researching?" I ask, feeling a little guilty that she was doing so much and I had passed out with my pants on.

Zooey snorts. "I wish." I don't think she's going to add anything to that, but then she says, "I was fighting with my mom."

"I *hate* fighting with my mom," I say quickly, squirming at even the thought. I'm debating asking her what they were fighting about. Does Zooey fight with her mom about things me and my mom disagree over? Whether sixth graders should have a bedtime, and washing my face when I'm too tired? I eye Zooey's perfect skin. I bet she never misses an opportunity to wash her face.

"Hey, Zooey!" a familiar voice says. We both turn to see Fee. My stomach flips at the sight of her, her dimple doing double-time as she practically skips over to us, grinning widely. "Here, this is for you," Fee says brightly, handing her a folded piece of paper.

"Thanks," Zooey says, though she doesn't sound that thankful.

"Sure!" Fee says shrilly. "No problem!"

"Anything else?" Zooey asks.

Fee's smile falters, and she shakes her head. Zooey walks away, not even saying good-bye to me. I have no choice but to awkwardly introduce myself to Fee, and walk with her to first period. It's weird. Zooey should be going, too, if she weren't walking in the opposite direction.

When we get to class, Fee sits down quickly and nods at the Ts, who look satisfied. And I watch Celeste whisper when she sees me walk by—"Who's that?"—and Fee's shrug and response. Celeste turns and blinks at me, offering a half smile. I smile back.

It's not until Ms. Clifton, my homeroom teacher, does roll call that I realize how weird my situation is. I'm on her roster; no other kids are turning around with "new girl" titters on their tongues. Celeste and Fee are the only ones in class who have no recollection of ever seeing me before. It's, like, not only is their memory blocked but so is the pathway into their brain that would take in information that would make them say, *Hey, why does everybody know this kid but we don't?*

This is going to be the longest day ever.

After three periods of the same thing, I am seriously wishing this school was large enough that I wouldn't have to see at least one of my friends in every single class.

I practically run to the library at lunch, sign in with Mr. Zubki, and hightail it to the Big Comfy Chair, hoping to nestle in and eat my lunch before I go online for more searching about the jinx. But once again, I see someone has taken it. The same pair of heavy-looking black lace-up boots hang over the arm.

I clear my throat. "Excuse me," I say sharply.

The person in the chair shifts, and a moment later, Zooey has tipped her head up into view and is smirking at me. "What?" she asks, swallowing a bit of whatever she's eating.

"Oh. It's you. You're, um . . . you're kind of hogging the Big Comfy Chair."

She tucks her head back into the little crook, crosses her legs the other way. "I got here first."

"You *always* get here first," I point out.

"I'm fast," she says, turning the page of her book and continuing to not look at me. "So yeah, I always get here first."

There is nothing for me to say to that. I sigh and turn, facing the thought of a lunch spent staring at the reflection of myself chewing a jelly sandwich in a blank computer screen.

"There are pillows," Zooey says. She nods toward the wall in front of the chair. "You can use those if you want."

"I thought we weren't friends," I say, my voice hard.

"It's a *pillow*," Zooey answers, "not a BFF necklace." I hesitate. "Look, go eat in front of a computer again if you want to; just seems kind of pathetic."

"You're the one hiding in a giant chair," I inform her.

"I'm not hiding," she says quickly.

"You could be sitting with Fee."

Zooey rolls her eyes.

"What do you have against her?" I ask. "You were kind of rude to her this morning."

Zooey shakes her head like I couldn't possibly understand. She finally says, "That girl is playing with fire." And goes back to reading her book.

"What do you mean?"

Zooey sighs. "Nothing."

I drop heavily onto a pillow, get out my lunch and Tilde's Realm #2, and start reading. "Hey," I say, eyeing her boots. "You weren't wearing those this morning, were you?"

Zooey gives me a quick glance, something like a smile flitting at the sides of her mouth, then goes back to her book. I guess I know now what she got when she turned in her ballet flats at the Popularity Dismissal Counter.

I read until I finish my sandwich, and then debate going over to the computers and searching for information on the jinx. I just don't know what I'll find. If anything.

It feels like the historical society is turning into my last and best hope.

So I stay on my pillow, reading. Sort of with Zooey, but sort of not.

It's actually not a one hundred percent horrible way to spend lunch.

chapter Fifteen

Oh, Saturday, how I love you!" I sigh to my ceiling when I wake up on Saturday morning. Having another day of being jinxed in front of you is much less depressing when that day will not be spent being ignored by your friends at school and spending a weirdly quiet lunch reading in close proximity to a girl who can spit fire. Actually . . . I had lunch with Zooey on Friday, too, and have to say those lunches were kind of the high points of the last couple of days. It was the only time in school that I didn't have a drumbeat of *BREAK THE JINX! BREAK THE JINX! BREAK THE JINX!* pounding in my ears, the only time I didn't feel like I was walking on eggshells and swallowing boulders that threatened to burst into sobs at any moment. It was thirty minutes of sweet relief, spent with a girl who has made it clear she doesn't give two hoots about me, outside of needing a warm body for our social studies project.

This weekend, though, I'm going to hang out with people who love me unequivocally and will shower me with attention: Salvatore Maletti and Martha Rowe. My parents. Dance floor sweethearts, New York City ex-pats, and the only people I plan on speaking to this whole weekend.

Except they're not home.

Dad has Saturday hours at the office, and a note left on the kitchen table downstairs tells me Mom is covering someone's shift at the hospital, so Champ and I have the house to ourselves. Actually, maybe being showered with attention isn't what I need. Maybe what I need is some "Hattie-Champ Quality Time!" We celebrate by playing Chase the Laser Pointer up and down all three floors of the house, and then sitting on the couch and eating Saturday Cereal and watching cartoons. Saturday Cereal is not to be confused with Other Days Cereal, because it has more sugar and sometimes even artificial coloring. Sometimes there are marshmallows! I eat two bowls and then have to lie down on the couch because that was just too many marshmallows.

Mom left me a Hattie-Do list along with her note, starting with washing my now grody and probably moldering field hockey uniform. I open the accordion door to our little laundry nook off the kitchen, half hoping that part of the jinx means my uniform has disappeared. No such luck. I shove it into the washing machine, turning my face away from the smell, and turn the dial to hot. I stand there listening to the water gush into the machine, thinking about the first time I wore the uniform. How I felt sort of embarrassed, sitting in the back of my parents' car on a Saturday just like this one, being driven to my first field hockey game, wearing a uniform. I can't even say that I looked the part, because I feel like I looked as wrong as I felt. My shin guards didn't feel right, and I was driving Dad crazy by ripping apart the Velcro and refastening it again and again as he drove through town. "You nervous, Hattie?" my mom asked. "This your first . . ." She paused.

"Sporting event of any kind?" I offered, giggling nervously.

"Hey, you played soccer," Dad said.

"I was three! And you didn't even have to kick the ball; you just had to not eat grass."

"You were so cute," Mom said, getting drippy with the memory. "You and Rae ignored what was going on and just played huggy-roll." It's true. There are pictures of the two of us hugging and tumbling on the ground and cracking up laughing.

"Man," I said, finally getting my shin guards on, "I would so much rather play huggy-roll." I saw Mom and Dad exchange a glance, and said quickly, "But I *love* field hockey, I really do."

And I do. I love every single part of it that does not involve actually playing or practicing or discussing field hockey. I love hanging out in the library with Fee and Piper before practice, and hanging out on the stone wall by the field waiting for our parents after practice. And I love the bus rides to away games, crammed into one seat with both Piper and Fee, cracking jokes and being silly. And I love halftime, when we suck the pulp out of fat slices of oranges.

One evening, coming back from a game that went longer than any field hockey game should ever go, Piper spread out on a seat and conked out, so it was just Fee and me sitting together.

"Tell me about Brooklyn, Hattie," Fee said.

I cleared my throat. "What do you want to know?"

"Everything," she said. I never know what to tell Fee when she asks me about New York. Nothing I say seems to be enough, nothing seems to fit the image she has of what life in the city is supposed to be.

"Well, we lived in this apartment . . ."

"With a doorman? Were you friends? Did he hail you cabs when you went out?"

"Um, no doorman."

She looked so disappointed, I said, "But Mr. Bakowski, our first-floor neighbor. He'd sign for packages and let the meter reader lady in when she came by."

This did not seem to impress her.

"But what'd you do for fun? You and . . ."

"Rae? We just did . . . I don't know, stuff. Hung out at the park." Reading Tilde's Realm.

"Shopping?"

"Sure!" I said. "We shopped sometimes."

"On Fifth Avenue? In those fancy stores?"

I thought hard. "Um . . . once we went to Saks to buy a dress for my cousin Gina's wedding," I offered. I didn't tell her I was six at the time. I kind of knew from the start that Fee's family has a lot of money, mostly because she told me. The first time I went to her house, she gave my mom and me a tour and told us how much everything cost. I know that if Fee lived in New York, she would probably have the kind of life she pictures for me. Lots of Broadway shows and summers in the Hamptons, that sort of thing.

"You're different than I thought," she said then. "I mean, when Piper told me she met this cool girl from New York City, I thought you'd be, like . . . different. Like, *cool* different. I was worried that Zooey and the Ts would want to, like, snatch you up."

I glanced over at Piper, so asleep her mouth gaped open. I wished she would wake up.

"But you're just like"—Fee furrowed her brow—"really normal. Just like us."

I shrugged, wanting to say, *But isn't that a good thing?*

And she said, "But you're GREAT!" so loudly that it woke up Piper, and the conversation ended.

The washing machine switches and starts to rock a little, bursting the bubble of my memory. I close the accordion doors and set to work on the rest of my mom's list. My memories can wait. I just hope I don't lose those, too.

chapter sixteen

Are you new here?" Piper's holding the front door of school open for me as I hurry inside. I missed the bus this morning, and Dad was cranky that he had to drop me off. Not the best start to a Monday. And now this. Again.

"Yep. New here," I say, catching my breath and following her inside. I push something down inside me, the something that would make it impossible to go through another conversation with Piper without crying. I just have to get through until tomorrow afternoon, when I can go to the historical society and find out how to break the jinx. The answer is there. It has to be.

"I can show you where the lockers are," Piper offers. "Do you have your number and combo?"

"Um, yes. I have it," I say weakly, cleaning off my steamed-up glasses as I follow her across the atrium floor. I glance toward the front office and see that the

Ts aren't sitting there. Their in-school suspension must be over.

"Where are you from?" Piper asks.

"Brooklyn," I answer. "New York."

"Cool!" she says, beaming. "My friend Fee is *obsessed* with New York."

"It's pretty great," I say. "Um, this is my locker."

"Well, see you later!"

"See you later."

I hear Celeste before I see her. "Pipes!" she says, and I turn and see her hurrying down the hall. I catch her eye for a second and she gives me a small smile before hurrying past me and linking arms with Piper.

"Hey!" Piper says to her. "How was ice time?" Except she says it, "Yice ti-yime!" and they both laugh.

"So good," Celeste says. "Nailed my lutz jump."

"Which one's that?" Piper asks. I watch as Fee pops out of the girls' bathroom and joins them.

"Oh, it's this one, right?" Fee asks, jumping and twirling.

Piper and Celeste applaud, and Celeste says, "I really wish you hadn't stopped skating."

Fee shrugs. "Wasn't my thing."

"Oof!" Someone bumps into me, hard, from behind. I swing around and find Teagan and Tess standing there, arms crossed over their chests. They must have stealth-walked out of the bathroom.

"What's your deal?" Teagan asks.

"Yeah, what's your deal?" Tess adds, earning a sharp look from Teagan.

I stifle a sigh. The few times I've been this close to the Ts, my heart has raced with nervousness. Now I just want to get to class.

"I don't have a deal," I answer.

"What's your deal with Zooey?" Teagan asks, more slowly this time.

"What do you mean?" My heart thrums in my ears.

"Why are you guys hanging out so much?"

"We're partners in social studies."

"At lunch?" Tess asks cattily, as if she's making a great point.

"Nice shirt," Teagan cuts in. I look down at today's cat T-shirt.

"Thanks," I say, raising my chin.

"Tell Zooey her time's running out," Teagan says.

"Apparently," I say, dropping onto a pillow in front of the Big Comfy Chair, "your time is running out."

Zooey looks up from her book. She beat me to the chair, again. "What do you mean?"

"I mean the Ts sent me with a message," I say solemnly. "Actually, two. First, they *really* like my shirt."

Zooey grins, snorts.

"Second, your time is running out."

"Ugh." She rolls her eyes. "They need to give it up."

"Give what up?"

She shakes her head like I couldn't possibly understand.

"Fine. Don't tell me," I say, getting out my own book. I'm on to my reread of Tilde's Realm #4.

"They want to be friends again," Zooey says.

I look at her. "And you don't?"

"You saw what they did to me. Why would I want to be friends with them?"

I shrug. "Because . . . they're Totally Popular? And they want to be friends with you?"

"Yeah, but we're not into the same things anymore."

"What, like, making people cry?"

I was joking, mostly, but Zooey actually looks hurt. "Exactly like making people cry."

"But you've always been friends with them . . ." She's giving me such a befuddled look as I ramble. "And they want to be friends with you. And why would you want to be friends with someone who didn't want to be friends with you? That would not make sense."

"That's ironic," she says drily.

"What?"

"Nothing. How was your weekend?"

I study her, trying to figure out what she means by "How was your weekend?" Is she being mean? I say, "Good. Yours?"

"Great," she says, lifting her chin. "I saw some camp friends. And it was exactly what I needed."

"What camp?"

"Camp Wohega."

I make a note to check it out when I get home.

"And," Zooey says, raising a foot, "I got new boots." They are a pretty royal blue, with laces all the way up her calf.

"I think the Ts are going to like those as much as they like my cat shirt," I say, and she smiles.

"If it isn't my women-in-colonial-times enthusiasts!" Maude says from behind the big green desk the next afternoon.

"Just wondering"—I have to push my voice out, I'm so afraid of Maude's answer—"if you've found something else about the jinx."

Maude is slunk down so low that her elbows resting on the sides of her chair have sent her shoulders up to her ears, making her neck disappear. She wears a black T-shirt that reads I AM SHER LOCKED, and purple leggings that seem to be covered in muppet fur. She doesn't answer me; she just swivels her chair from side to side, staring at us.

"What are you doing?" Zooey asks her.

"Swiveling," Maude says. "It helps me think." With one final swivel that sends her around in a full circle, she plants her motorcycle boots with a heavy thud onto the wood floor to stop the rotation. "I did just so happen to find something about the jinx."

"Oh my God," I say, my voice quivering. "Really? About how to break it?"

"Did you *not* just hear her call us Colonial Women Enthusiasts?" Zooey asks. "We have a title now; we can't just change our project."

"Just curious," I murmur, watching as Maude slips a thin volume from one of the cavernous drawers in the desk and hands it to me.

As she hands me the book, I look at her questioningly, too nervous to open it.

"You take the rectangular object," Maude says slowly, "and you open it up . . . and look!" Her voice rises in faux excitement. "This page is called the table of contents. Isn't it cute!"

Despite my anticipation, I manage to shoot her a smirk as I open to the table of contents.

It lists first an introduction, and then chapters on the history of Trepan's Grove. And then, halfway down

the page, *Chapter Six: Poem: The Harvest Jinx . . . . . 43*.
I flip through the book with shaking fingers, page 41,
42, 45.

"Where is it?" I whisper, flipping back. It's then that I
see the torn half page and the words at the top. My eyes
scan the words, once, twice, three times, trying to understand what I'm reading:

> Every year at Harvesttime is the moment to
>   remind
> That what you say and what you mean should
>   have nothing in between.
> All twenty-four hours of Festival Day,
> Be aware of what you say,
> For make a promise before you think,
> And you could get a Harvest Jinx.
> A jinx will last 'til the New Year dawns
> One minute past midnight, and it will be gone.

And there the poem gets cut off, the bottom of the
page ripped off.

"Wait," I say desperately, flipping the page over, hoping maybe there will be more of the poem on the back,
even if the bottom half of the page is gone. But the back of
the page is blank, and the next page starts a new chapter
on the food served at the bicentennial celebration.

My stomach drops. "That's it? Someone ripped out the page?"

"People are the worst," Maude announces.

I make a sound like *"GAH!"* and read the poem again.

"Dude, you have to relax," Zooey says. "We found more of the poem than anyone's seen in a long time. We can still find a way to include it in our paper, okay?"

I don't respond but ask Maude, "There has to be another copy of this book, though, right? One that has the whole poem?" The thought of over two more months of living under the jinx is more than I can bear. "Can we look it up? We have the title."

"Oh, I looked it up," Maude says, "and this is the only copy. Someone made it for the historical society, as a gift after the bicentennial. But it's interesting, yes? Now we know how long this mythical jinx business is supposed to last. Just until New Year's Eve."

"But . . ."

"Sorry, kid," Maude says, her voice sounding far away as I slowly turn and walk toward the stairs.

Zooey sounds practically underwater when she calls sarcastically, "Guess I'll just keep on working! Thanks for your help!"

I'm a zombie through dinner. Mom feels my head. Dad makes me stick out my tongue. They send me to bed early and I don't even object. I slump up the stairs to my room and stare at the calendar on my wall.

I fill the rest of the year with *J*'s. Rows and rows of them. I press so hard, the soft tip of the red marker flattens and splits, so the last *J*'s, in December, are huge, sloppy shapes. Then I take a black marker and cross out the days that have already passed since I was first jinxed. I'll do this every day, until all the days are *X*'d out, until I'm free.

chapter seventeen

This is my new normal, I think dully, unzipping my coat as I slog up the steps of the school bus the next day.

I take the bus to school.

I slog through the wet leaves in the courtyard.

I wipe my fogged-up glasses and my runny nose.

I stuff my giant coat in my miniature locker.

I walk to first period.

I walk past Fee and Celeste, who do not look at me. They don't look at each other, either.

Fee's bangs look somehow even shorter today, and she's wearing an ill-fitting dress in a color that makes me think of dirty diapers. She has her chin raised, staring straight ahead. Celeste looks like she's going to cry.

Look ahead, Hattie, I tell myself, moving to the back of the class.

I take my seat and see that Zooey is staring at Fee,

her lips parted a little, her eyes wide. She looks . . . sad. And then she looks angry.

I look away. It's no concern of mine. I'm a lone wolf. I'm going to do my time with the jinx, and then it will be broken.

I don't have to talk to anyone during first period. Or second. Or lunch . . .

"What is your major malfunction?"

"Excuse me?" I look up, snapped out of my lone-wolf state.

Zooey is giving me a hard stare. "You've been, like, dragging your chin around school all day. What's wrong?"

I didn't consider this. I actually thought Zooey and I could just go on eating lunch and basically ignoring each other for the rest of the school year, until my jinx is over.

"Nothing's wrong," I answer.

She scoffs. "Right." She pauses for a long moment and then says, "So . . . what are you reading?"

"This?" I ask, holding up my book for her to see. "Tilde's Realm."

"My big brother loves those," Zooey says. I smile. And she continues. "But he's a nerd."

I drop my smile, open the book again.

"Relax!" Zooey says, laughing. "I'm joking. I call him a nerd, he calls me a plastic. It's our thing. Are you excited

161

for the last book to come out? Just before Christmas, right?"

I nod. "I'm on a waiting list." I hesitate, not wanting her to make fun of me, but add, "My parents tried to convince me I should wait until Christmas to read it so they could give it to me as The Best Present Ever, but there is no way that's going to happen."

"My parents tried the same thing with my brother." Zooey laughs. "I have a little brother, too. Ryan. He's in second grade."

"Oh, with Peanut Packenbush?" I say, wondering if I am somehow tempting the jinx to get worse.

Zooey snorts. "My little brother loves that girl."

"So"—I try to remember—"were you at the Harvest Festival? Did you see him perform in the pageant?"

Zooey presses her lips together and breathes in through her nose. "No. I wasn't feeling well that day."

I nod, sensing there is more to the story, but also sensing that she doesn't really want to say it.

"My parents took a video," Zooey says, "and Ryan and I watch it, like, every morning. He says it's because he wants me to see him sing, but I think it's because he wants to look at Peanut."

She gets so quiet that I try to think of something to say. "I'm an only child," I finally offer. "But I have, like, two hundred cousins."

She nods.

"And like fifty percent of them are named Gina."

Zooey laughs.

I hesitate a second before saying, "Can I ask you something?"

She nods.

"Why do you sit in here every day? I mean, couldn't you sit with the, like . . . Upper Popular people?"

"I'm on hiatus from all that," Zooey responds.

"Me too."

"I noticed."

"But . . . why? I mean, so what if the Ts disowned you. That doesn't mean you have to go into hiding."

"Not hiding, hi—"

"Hiatus. I know, but it just seems extreme."

Zooey sighs. "People in this town don't change, Hattie. You'll realize that. They don't change, and they won't let you change, either. Sometimes you just have to, like . . . opt out of everything if you want to be anything other than what they want you to be."

"So you don't want to be popular?" I ask.

"I don't want to be *mean*," she says.

"Oh," I say, surprised. I thought being mean was Zooey's thing. From the stories I heard, she kind of enjoyed it. But since this is the second time she's mentioned it, I guess maybe she's serious.

"Why do *you* sit here every day?"

It's not like I didn't expect her to ask me the same question I'd asked her. I just don't have an answer that wouldn't result in the jinx getting worse. So I go for a non-committal shrug. "I'm on hiatus, too."

She studies me shrewdly. "You can tell me about it, you know. I'm a good listener. I was the head camper at camp. That's, like, basically a junior counselor. All the girls came to me with their problems."

"Maybe someday," I say.

"All right. Keep your secrets . . . Moving on. Our topic is due to Ms. Lyle next Wednesday. I have to watch my brother after school tomorrow, so do you want to meet up at the historical society again Tuesday night, just to see if there's anything else there?"

"Yeah, right."

"What?"

"Two things. First, that will be Halloween. Don't you have to, like, scare little children or something?"

"Ha-ha. That's my night off," she says drily. "Next?"

"Well . . . you're making plans as if we're not going to see each other here basically every day from now until then."

Zooey shrugs. "Well, one of us might tire of the library before Tuesday. So I like to have things nailed down."

"Oh, I am here *all year*," I say with a laugh. "No way I'm leaving."

Chapter Eighteen

Where's the glossy one?" Maude asks next Tuesday, stepping out from between the bookshelves and making me jump. I look up from the book I'm reading, *The History of Trepan's Grove*. The gilded hands of the clock hanging crooked from a rafter over us read 5:45 p.m.

"I guess she's not coming," I answer, closing the book I just finished and adding it the stack. I have to say I'm a little bummed.

"She stood you up?" Maude asks, sitting down cross-legged on the cushion next to me, and setting down the almost-empty bottle of purple Fizzy Fuzz I brought for her when I arrived.

I shrug. "I guess? Maybe she changed her mind and went to a Halloween party or something."

"Not you, though?" Maude asks.

"I have work to do," I respond. "You know, colonial women and all that."

"Hm," Maude says.

"Wait," I say, thinking of something. "Don't you have people to hang out with? I mean, I bet kids from your grade are in town this weekend."

"I'm sure they are. That doesn't mean I'm going to call them."

"Why not?"

"It's complicated."

I narrow my eyes at her.

"What?" she asks.

"I'm just trying to decide if you're old enough to say 'It's complicated.' That's one of those things parents say when they don't want to bother explaining something to you."

"Exactly," she says, looking satisfied.

There is a ruckus beyond the bookshelves, and we both look up as Zooey emerges.

"Sorry I'm late," she says, dropping her stuff. "I had to go home and help Ryan with his Halloween costume because my mom was running late. What's up?"

"We didn't think you were coming," Maude says.

Zooey flashes me an offended look. "I told you I'd be here, and I am. And"—she shifts into a grin—"I brought treats!" From behind her back, she produces an orange plastic jack-o'-lantern bowl full of Halloween candy and plops down on the floor, nudging the candy bowl toward Maude and me.

✳ ✳ ✳

An hour later, we are all sprawled out on the oversize pillows in the little nook. I'm on my belly, chewing on a Starburst and silently lamenting the lack of anything in any of these books having to do with jinx breaking. Maude is beside me, on her back, one leg crossed over the other, nearing the end of her book on string theory. Zooey lies on the other side on her belly, writing down notes in her notebook from what she's reading.

Maude's the one who looks at the clock and says, "Whoa, it's past seven. I've got to close up. Management hasn't approved overtime."

"I kind of thought my first Halloween in Trepan's Grove would be more . . . Halloweeny."

"How do you mean?" Zooey asks.

I sit up. "I don't know. In the city, we would trick-or-treat at the stores on the avenue, or if you had a friend who lived in a fancy apartment building, like my friend Rae, you could trick-or-treat in there. I always wanted to do the sort of trick-or-treating you see in the movies, going house to house with a bunch of other kids. This town seems made for that, especially around the common."

"Why don't you two go out with your school chums?" Maude asks, standing and doing a theatrical stretch.

167

Zooey reaches out to nudge the bowl of candy toward me. "I'm on social hiatus."

"And I'm between friends," I add.

We both look over at Maude, who, looking surprised to be put on the spot, shrugs and says, "Speak for yourselves. I have a rich and robust social life outside of the historical society. I'm just . . ."

"On hiatus?" Zooey asks.

"Between friends?" I offer.

There's this, like . . . moment, this silent beat, and then we all start cracking up laughing. Maude and I laugh so hard we have to take our glasses off, which makes Zooey howl, but then—get this—it turns out Zooey's a snort laugher! And the first time she does it, it's this little delicate snort that would maybe come out of a cartoon piglet wearing a tutu, but it's still so shocking that everybody just FREEZES for a second. Zooey claps a hand over her mouth, her eyes wide and totally horrified, and then she starts, like, quaking and then sucks in this ENORMOUS snort that sends us all into hysterics.

"Come with me," Maude says, wiping her eyes and sliding her glasses back on. We follow her between the bookshelves, over the long rug, and down another set of bookshelves, each of us still bursting out with giggles every so often. Maude leads us to a small closet in the back corner of the attic and opens it to reveal rows of hanging black garments encased in plastic. "One of the churches stores their choir robes here," she says.

Which is why, twenty minutes later, the three of us are picking up the hems of our long black robes as we trot up the front steps of the pretty purple house across from the Chin statue. Zooey reaches out and rings the bell, and we stand there giggling until a woman answers the door and tips her head to the side as she examines us.

We look back at her in silence until one of us remembers to shout, "Oh! Trick or treat!"

"And who might you be?" she asks, her face a combo of amused and disapproving as she drops a single mini chocolate candy into the blue paper Trading Post bags Trudy gave us downstairs, on the condition that we return with Reese's Peanut Butter Cups for her.

"We're Ruth Bader Ginsburg," Maude says in her low voice, straightening the white paper-towel collar around her neck.

The woman blinks at us, and then cracks up. "Well, in that case!" and she plunks down a handful of candy in each of our bags.

We weave in and out of joyful crowds of costumed kids all much younger than us and hit every single one of the houses up one side of the common, until we get to the white-trimmed gray house at the very top. Its windows are aglow from the first wide picture windows to the gable on the fourth floor, where Piper and I used to sit and stare out at the common, waiting for something interesting to happen.

"I'll do it," Zooey says, moving by me, even though it's my turn to ring the bell.

Piper opens the door, wearing a very faded Captain America costume, takes one look at us, and shouts, "MOM, IT'S A WHOLE BUNCH OF RUTH BADER GINSBURGS!" She opens the door wider and I see Ms. Packenbush leaning over the kitchen island, a pile of paperwork in front of her. She looks down the hall toward the front door, then lifts her reading glasses to the top of her head and lets out a whoop of laughter. In a moment, she's standing in front of us with her phone, taking a million pictures, saying she wants to show the students in her law class tomorrow.

Then she looks more closely at us and for a second I think, *She is going to remember me!* but she says, "Maude! I didn't know you were in town! Piper, go get your sister. Paola would love to see you!"

Piper disappears and I look after her, see a scary movie paused on the television in their cozy den, the outline of Celeste's curly hair lit up by her phone as she types into it.

I can tell by the tilt of her head and the way she's pressing hard that she's angry about something. Piper returns a moment later with her older sister Paola, who has her hair pulled up in a messy ponytail and is wearing a pair of pink-striped long johns that would probably fit her younger sister perfectly but make Paola look like her long limbs are about to bust out of them.

"MAUDE!" Paola shouts, pulling her into a hug. "Holy crow, it's been YEARS!"

Maude looks completely at a loss as she pulls away from Paola's hug. She finally says in a low voice, "I've been away."

Paola says, "Oh, Maudlin!" and it sounds like she is halfway between laughing and crying. "I've missed you! Do you want to come up? Oh my gosh, Petra is going to DIE when she finds out I saw you!"

Throughout this whole exchange, Zooey and I are standing there awkwardly in our scratchy paper-towel collars, holding our bags of candy. It is so weird to see someone be so friendly and affectionate with Maude. I realize I'd never seen her interact with anyone outside of me and Zooey.

"Hey, Zooey," Piper says. "Do you and your friend want to come in?" She gives me a small smile and my heart leaps. *YES! Yes, I do want to come in! Even if you don't remember me.*

Zooey makes an angry sound in her throat and says tightly, "That's all right. We've got some more houses to hit." I blink at her but realize it would be kind of weird if I stayed without her, so I mumble good-bye to Piper, give one last longing look inside her adorable house, and follow Zooey down the steps.

"You didn't want to stay?" I ask when I catch up.

"Nope," she says as we join a pack of witches crossing to the other side of the common.

"Why not?" I ask, an odd feeling in my stomach.

She swings around to face me, and the pack of witches trots up the front walk of a tall house, leaving us alone under a streetlamp. "Why would *you* want to stay? She barely said a word to you."

I'm caught off guard by the question. "Just thought it would be fun, that's all."

Zooey makes a snorting sound, but not like the one she makes when she's laughing. "Fun. Right." We step aside so the returning witches can pass, and walk silently up the path. It's not as fun this time to tell the person at the door who we are. I think it's our lack of enthusiasm that makes the man say, "A little old for this, aren't you, ladies?"

When we get back to the sidewalk, Zooey says, "Look, I'm trying to make it a point not to be friends with people who are jerks. I think you should, too."

"Piper's not a jerk," I say, my lower lip quivering. I wish I could tell Zooey the truth. I really do.

Her anger seems to deflate a bit. "Everyone's a jerk sometimes, Hattie."

Things are a little icy between us until we get to the Dentist's House, where my mom and dad are chatting and laughing on the front porch with the couple who owns the house next door, a bowl of colorful toothbrushes wrapped in cellophane on the railing. There is a giant coffeepot full of hot cider, a stack of paper cups next to it on a wooden side table. Mom's dressed up like a witch, and Dad has taken his gorilla mask off so he's just an exceptionally furry-except-his-face dude.

He comes loping over to us, making a gorilla face and grunting, pretending to pick a bug from Zooey's hair and eating it. She laughs, even lets out a little snort.

"Ugh, *Dad*!" I groan.

Zooey gives me a sideways *It's okay* smile and puts her arm around me as we pose against the railing for pictures.

chapter Nineteen

Hey!" I say excitedly to Zooey the next morning, hurrying to her desk just before Ms. Lyle closes the door. I slip a
copy of our proposal on her desk. We'd written most of it
at the historical society, but I volunteered to read it over
again last night and make sure everything was in shape.
Zooey looks it over and grins. "Good job."

"You too!"

I walk quickly to my seat at the back of the room,
wrinkling my brow for a moment when I see Fee and
Celeste turned slightly away from each other, not
talking. It is a weird sight, because the two of them may
bicker, but I've never seen them actually stay mad at
each other. It's not until Ms. Lyle announces it's time
to read our proposals out loud that I figure out what's
going on.

"Celeste and Fee? Which of you would like to read
your proposal?"

Celeste shoots Fee an angry look and says, "We're not ready, Ms. Lyle."

"Why?"

"Um . . ." Fee says. "I was sick last night." Her eyes keep glancing over toward Teagan and Tess, and I cringe for her. She wants their approval, even for this. "So we couldn't finish." I guess that's why Fee wasn't at Piper's house last night.

"Speak to me after class," Ms. Lyle says sharply. "Moving on. Next!"

When it's Zooey's and my turn, I nod at her and she reads our proposal out loud. Teagan and Tess snicker, because that is apparently the only thing they are capable of doing when Zooey speaks now.

Ms. Lyle listens to it with her arms crossed, a firm look on her face. When Zooey is done, she sits down, but Ms. Lyle continues to study her. Finally, she says in her paper-flutter voice, "So you're going to focus your research on colonial women?"

We both nod.

Ms. Lyle gives a wry smile. "Intriguing. I look forward to what you'll find."

Zooey swings around and we exchange a victorious smile.

When class gets out, Zooey waits for me at the classroom door. "Nice job," I say. "I always get too nervous reading aloud in class."

"I love it," Zooey says, laughing.

"Ouch!" I say, stepping back when one of the Ts steps on my toes as the two girls shove their way between Zooey and me, so close that my nose is basically on top of Tess's head.

"Where were you last night, Zooey?" Teagan asks.

Wait, *what*? I thought Zooey wanted nothing more to do with the Ts anymore. Why would they think she was going over to Teagan's house?

Tess crosses her arms, the motion making her knock into me even more. I step back, out of the way. She adds, "Yeah. Where were you?"

Zooey meets my confused gaze through the space between their heads for a moment, then looks back to Teagan.

"I told you. I had work to do," she says firmly.

"Well, my mom thought you were coming," Teagan says.

Zooey actually looks a little troubled by this. "I never said—"

"Yeah," Tess says, "Teagan's mom totally freaked out on her."

Zooey looks at me again, gives a very slight shake of her head.

"Oh!" I say, so loudly that both Teagan and Tess glance over their shoulders at me. "I have to go to class." They both turn back to Zooey, and I walk away, leaving her to have a low, tense conversation with the Ts.

Zooey catches up with me just before the classroom door. "Hey," I say, "what was that all about?"

She presses her lips together, and then lets out a huge sigh. "Teagan's mom keeps trying to get us all to be friends again."

"Really?" I ask, surprised at this tidbit of insider information.

"She's not doing it to be nice," Zooey says bitterly. "She's doing it because it doesn't look good for her precious kid to be a bully. If we become friends again, she can just tell the principal that 'the girls had a little fight' and get the suspension erased from her record."

"Wowza," I say, shuddering a little. "That's intense."

"You don't know the half of it," Zooey says, but then she presses her lips together. "I feel weird gossiping about it." She gives a long glance down the hall where Teagan and Tess are walking away. "I mean, we *were* friends once upon a time."

I give her an exaggerated approving look. "That is really, really Zooey 2.0 of you."

Zooey shrugs, but smiles. "I told you. I'm totally good at listening. I won't blab their secrets, and I wouldn't tell yours, either."

She waits for me to say something, and I desperately want to be able to tell her about the jinx, but I don't. I just smile and say, "Good to know!"

chapter twenty

Something kind of shifts after Halloween. It's not that I, like, embrace being jinxed or something, but I start to feel a little okay about it. It's two weeks until Thanksgiving, and then five more weeks until New Year's, and then the jinx will break and I'll be free.

And now that I've discovered that Zooey isn't the coal-hearted witch I'd thought she was, the next seven weeks aren't going to be totally terrible. I mean, it still totally stinks that my friends don't remember me, but there is nothing I can do about it, so why spend the next two months yearning after them and choking on panic whenever we happen to talk to each other?

I mean, seriously, that's no way to live.

So I just sort of relax about it all. And I actually start to look forward to talking to my old friends, even though they never remember our conversations the next day. Piper especially. I get into the habit of being late to first period so I can be by my locker when she comes hurrying into school. If it's raining out, she'll fall like a baby deer on ice when she skids to a stop at her locker. If it's dry, her skinny fingers are twirling the combination before her body even comes to a full stop.

"Hi!" I'll say, happy just to be chatting with her. "I'm Hattie. I'm new here."

"Oh, hi!" she always says, breathless from her run inside. Sometimes she'll say, "I'm Piper, and I am l-a-t-e!" Or sometimes she'll say, "Oh, hey! Where are you from?" And then when I tell her, she'll tell me all about Fee and how she's obsessed with Brooklyn.

And Celeste is the friendliest to me she's ever been when she meets me for the first time every day. I'll always ask about her skating sweatshirt, and she'll always get super excited telling me about her team and the rink. One day, though, she's actually kind of grumpy when I meet her again for the first time. "Are you okay?" I ask. I know it's forward, but she won't remember it tomorrow anyway, so who cares. Celeste nods and focuses her gaze somewhere over my left shoulder. "Don't get me wrong, I love my little half brother. But I sometimes wish my mom hadn't just dropped him in my lap and assumed we'd get along. I would have liked some choice in the matter." She laughs, then says, "Not sure what choice I had, though. No thank you, please put him back in your belly?" She shakes off what, for her, passes as a melancholy mood and asks, "So where'd you move here from?"

As for Fee, I just can't figure her out. She's acting more and more strangely every day, and I barely ever see her with Celeste and Piper. She's always wearing weird clothes and garish makeup, and she seems really, really nervous. I wish so much I could ask Piper and Celeste what's going on. Because, honestly, I'm getting worried. I wish there was something I could do.

chapter twenty-one

Homework doesn't stop for the jinx, and Zooey and I have been hard at work on our project. We've gone to the town library a couple of times, but our favorite research place is definitely the historical society.

"You'll want to leave that on," Maude calls from behind the green desk as I unzip my heavy coat at the top of the stairs. She's got her jacket on, and a hat. So does Zooey, who managed to beat me here. She turns to look at me from one of the creaky leather chairs in front of the desk, and then turns back to face Maude. Something feels . . . off.

"What's up?" I ask, sitting in the matching chair next to Zooey.

"The glossy one is worried about you," Maude says.

I look at Zooey in amused confusion, expecting her to make some noise of objection, but instead she says, "The smart one is right. I'm worried about you. You've been acting . . . more bizarre than usual."

I tilt my head. Bizarre? I've been happy. Sort of at peace with the whole jinx thing. I meet my old friends every day, they forget me, and then we do it again the next day. Things are fine. Well, as fine as they can be if you're jinxed. I'm not sure how to respond, and settle for a school-yard-toned "So?"

"So . . . I feel like I keep trying to find out what's going on with you, and you don't talk to me even though we eat lunch together every day."

I half laugh, half huff. "We talk every day!"

"Yeah, we talk," she says, sounding frustrated. "But not about anything real. I mean, on your part anyway. I told you all about what happened with the Ts, and you don't say a word about why you eat lunch in the library every day."

"I like books."

"*I* like books," Maude interjects, "and even I get tired of their lunchtime company."

I turn to Zooey. "You haven't told me everything about you and the Ts! You just said you wanted to stop being mean."

Zooey blinks at me, like I am being somehow unbelievable. "You want me to tell you *more*? When you haven't told me anything about what's going on with you? I mean, what do your parents think?" she asks. "Aren't they worried that you're not, like, hanging out with anyone else after school or anything? *My* mom's even worried about you!"

"Your mom?" I ask, surprised. "You told your mom about me?"

"Of course I told her about you! I hang out with you every day, but I know, like, nothing about you. She wants to call your mom and talk, but I told her I'd talk to you first."

"She can't call my mom!"

"Why?" Zooey asks flatly. "What's going on?"

"Because they don't know that I've been . . ." I hesitate, looking for a non-jinx-related word. "Eating in the library, so to speak."

"WHAT?" Maude's voice actually gets squeaky.

"What *what*?" I shoot back. "What's the big deal? I eat in the library. Big whoop-dee-do!"

"Yeah, but you don't whoop-dee-*do* anything else!" Zooey says. "You're like . . . a hermit."

"And you're not?" I snap back.

"I have friends!" Zooey says. "They're from . . ."

"Camp. I know," I say, rolling my eyes.

"Don't make fun!" Zooey says, sounding younger than I've heard her before. "Camp is the best thing that's ever happened to me!"

"Getting off point," Maude says in a low sing-song.

"You have to talk to your parents!" Zooey practically yells at me. "And me, too. You have to talk to me. You have to tell me what's going on with you!"

I wish, so much, that I could tell her. But I can't risk making the jinx worse. So I tell her something that has nothing to do with the jinx, something I might not have realized until I blurt it out.

"I'm homesick. For Brooklyn. And I haven't told my parents because I don't want them to feel bad for moving me here."

"So they feel bad," Zooey says. "So what? They're grown-ups; they know how to deal with it."

"And they would feel worse if they knew you were keeping this all inside," Maude says.

"I guess you're right," I say.

"And us," Zooey says. "I mean, you don't have to, like, share everything, but some things."

"Okay," I say, a weight lifting off my chest. And I feel that I should say something right here, right now. Some truth I haven't shared.

"I'm kind of a nerd," I finally announce, my voice shaking a little.

Maude and Zooey exchange yet another look. Zooey says, "Yeah, we kind of picked up on that."

"No," I say, "like, I really like that series . . ."

"Tilde's Realm?" Maude asks. "We know."

"You read it every day in the library," Zooey adds. "And we've actually talked about it. Remember, my older brother likes it, too?"

"And I like cat T-shirts."

"Yeah, and striped leggings. I've noticed," Zooey says. "Why would that be some sort of secret?"

I give her an incredulous look and blurt out, "Are you kidding? You're telling me we'd be friends if we weren't, like, forced to hang out because neither of us has anywhere to go besides the library and this place?"

"For your information," Zooey says icily, after a long moment of silence, "I don't *have* to eat in the library."

"Oh," I say. Then, "Really?"

"Really," Zooey says firmly.

"Oh," I say again. If Zooey was willing to accept me just the way I am, why had I assumed my real friends wouldn't?

chapter twenty-two

Sharing with Maude and Zooey has me feeling so good that I'm determined to talk to my parents at dinner. I just can't figure out quite what to say. I'm so deep in thought that I don't notice they've both stopped eating. My mom is gripping my dad's hand so hard her knuckles have turned white, and they are both looking at me.

"Hattie," my dad says seriously. "You have to talk to us, honey. You've been acting strange for weeks, and you keep saying you're fine, but, hon, we can tell you're not fine."

It's obvious they think they are going to have to coax the truth out of me, but I just blurt out, "I know I've been acting strange, but I've been really homesick for Brooklyn. It's been hard living here without a close friend like Rae. But I've made friends now, with Zooey and Maude, and things are already getting so much better."

"Oh," my mom says. Then she stage-whispers to my dad, "Can we still eat the ice cream we bought to bribe her into spilling her guts?"

Here's what I learn that my parents miss about Brooklyn, over ice-cream sundaes. Mom misses the farmers' markets, the free summer outdoor dance performances, taking the East River Ferry to Governor's Island on summer days, being able to find delicious food from all around the world, and being able to buy almost everything at small, locally owned businesses. Dad misses taking the subway to work because it gave him almost an hour a day to read, record stores that sell actual records, and meeting his fellow Boston ex-pats at a bar to watch Red Sox games. I tell them I miss Rae, Rae, and more Rae. "So call her," Mom says, like it's the most obvious thing in the world. I nod, like I fully plan on taking her advice. But I haven't texted or talked to her since the weekend I got jinxed. It's been so long, I just don't know what to say.

When I go up to bed that night and write my giant X over today's date, I vow that as soon as this jinx mess is done, I'm going to call Rae. And, after talking with my parents, I know that getting through the rest of the year isn't going to do me in.

What follows are two weeks that are actually one hundred percent pretty okay.

Zooey and I keep meeting for lunch in the library, I'm still reading Tilde's Realm, wanting to reread the whole series before the last book comes out in December. But I'm not just reading. We're talking a lot of the time, too. And Mr. Zubki steps into our little space one day to inform us that if we're going to be here every day, he's going to put us to work. So a couple of days a week, we shelve books for him and even get to put those crinkly covers on new books that come in. I had no idea Zooey was such a crazy reader. I mean, she doesn't read fantasy the way I do, but show her any books about real kids in real situations, she will stop what she's doing and start reading.

I'm not sure when exactly our friendship moves from just lunch and the historical society to the world outside, but soon we're waiting for each other after class, and even going over to each other's houses. We still see Maude twice a week, and even though we keep asking her to hang out with us on days that don't start with *T*, she refuses. She finally says that she indeed has renewed a friendship with an older school chum, none other than Paola Packenbush, and has been hanging out at Chez Packenbush most weekends when Paola is home. Zooey and I discuss this at length and decide it's a good thing she has a friend besides us.

Each week, I cross out more and more *J*'s on my calendar. On Thanksgiving, my mom invites Zooey's parents and her brothers over for dessert, and Zooey joins my cousins and me in the den, watching movies while the adults talk and laugh and make a ton of noise.

chapter twenty-three

The first week in December, Zooey texts me that she is staying home because she has a stomach bug. After sending her a series of grossly funny barfing emojis, I realize that this will be the first time in a long time that I'll be eating lunch by myself.

"I'd like an update on your reports," Ms. Lyle says at the beginning of class. "Just so I can be sure you are on target to have them completed before the holiday recess."

Some pairs are better off than others. Darren and Jacob appear to be almost done, while a few others seem to think Ms. Lyle will not notice they haven't even really gotten started.

When she calls on me, Celeste and Fee turn around in curiosity. I watch the words *new kid* form on Fee's mouth.

"Ms. Maletti, would you like to wait until Zooey has returned to update us?" Ms. Lyle asks.

"No, that's okay," I answer. "I have our notes."

"Go ahead, then. How is your research?" A little smile plays on her thin lips.

"Great!" I say, blushing because I sound so excited. "Oh, also! We actually found part of the complete Harvest Jinx poem at the historical society."

Ms. Lyle blinks at me. "The complete poem?"

"Well, almost." I explain, "Not just the 'Make a promise before you think, and you could get a Harvest Jinx' part, but some of what comes after it."

I don't think she realizes she's shuffle-stepped over to my desk until she lightly presses her papery fingertips on my hand where it rests on my book. "You've read the rest of the poem?"

My classmates look about as confused by Ms. Lyle's attention as I feel, especially Fee and Celeste, who assume this is my first day of school.

"Um, not the whole poem," I explain. "Just maybe half of it. The rest was torn out of the book we found it in."

"Ah," she says, the flat line of her mouth curving up into an unfamiliar smile. "You found the book."

The bell rings just as I'm asking her, "What book?" I am sure she hears my question, but she moves back up the aisle to the front of the class, announcing that everyone else can give their updates on their projects tomorrow.

I linger by her desk after class, but she busies herself sorting a neat pile of paper into a different neat pile of paper on the other side of her desk, one piece at a time.

"Ms. Lyle?" I finally say when it's obvious that she is going to keep on ignoring me.

"Yes, Hattie?" Her eyes seem huge through her glasses.

"What did you mean by 'you found the book'?"

She looks down at the piece of paper she is moving from stack to stack. "I meant that it was nice that you found the poem in a book."

"But"—I wait for her hand to move from one pile to the next—"you didn't say *a* book, you said *the* book."

"Did I?" She looks up at me in surprise. "I suppose I misspoke." She glances behind me, toward the clock on the wall. "You are going to be late for lunch, Ms. Maletti."

I head to the library, as usual, and offer to help Mr. Zubki even though I could finally get a chance to sit in the Big Comfy Chair, since Zooey isn't here. It feels weird to be in our little area without her. Mr. Zubki puts me to work helping him shelve books in the history section. With the whole sixth grade working on our projects, which are due before the holiday break, he says a lot of books have been going in and out.

"Mr. Zubki, do you know how long Ms. Lyle has taught here?" I ask him.

"Oh, she was here long before I started," Mr. Zubki responds.

"Did she grow up here?"

He gives me a quizzical look. "This is one of those moments when it would be better for you to use a primary source."

I nod, even though I have a feeling Ms. Lyle isn't going to be too open to talking about her personal life.

"Why do you ask?" he asks.

"Just curious, I guess."

Zooey's out again the next day, which means that in the afternoon, I'll be hanging out with Maude by myself. But first, I need to get through the school day without the one person at school I consider to be a friend.

At lunch I start to wander my usual way down to the library, but as I do, I pass Celeste and Piper on the way to the cafeteria. I "met" them both this morning, so they smile when they pass. I pause after they go into the cafeteria, and I see Fee's already there, waiting for them. Her clothes have gotten even more bizarre, and I heard someone say that she got called down to guidance the other day because you could see her underwear through her skirt.

I make the decision before I even realize it, and soon I am striding into the cafeteria after Piper and Celeste. I walk slowly, to give them a chance to sit down and for Piper to pull out her ONLY NUT ALLOWED sign. When I get closer, I sense some iciness between Celeste and Fee, and watch as Piper looks distressed at the tension between her friends.

"Hi," I say, standing at the head of the table. My stomach jumps, a happy sort of nervousness.

"Oh, hi!" Piper says, like she's happy for something to break the tension. "How was your first day?"

I nod. "Great! Okay if I sit here?"

"Sure," Celeste says. Piper moves over, making room next to her for me to sit.

"So where are you from?" Fee asks. She's wearing makeup, a sort of cat's-eye eyeliner that I'm frankly surprised her mom let her leave the house with.

"Brooklyn," I answer, and her eyes go wide. "Have you ever been?"

She shakes her head. "I want to, though, so badly. What's it like?"

Usually, when Fee would ask me, I'd feel put on the spot, like nothing I say could have been as great as what she imagined. But this time, since she'll forget all of this tomorrow, I want to answer honestly. I take a second to think of what to say. "It was the best. I loved my neighborhood, and my school. There were always kids around, in our building, on our block, at the park, wherever.

We lived on the top floor of this old apartment house with a view of the Statue of Liberty. And I had a best friend named Rae. We read a lot of that fantasy series Tilde's Realm together."

It's a random list of facts, but Fee looks entranced. She blinks at me. "You look kind of familiar."

"What?" I ask so forcefully that she almost reels back, gives her head a shake.

"Nothing," she says brightly after a moment. "So where do you live now?"

I'm still puzzling over this when I climb the stairs to the historical society that afternoon. It seemed, for just a moment, like Fee recognized me. It strikes me that it's not until I actually told the whole truth about myself and my life in Brooklyn that she thought I was someone worth impressing.

"How's the glossy one?" Maude asks when I get up the stairs.

"Still barfing, I think. Hey, do you know Ms. Lyle, who teaches English and social studies at school?"

"I do," Maude says, not looking up from her book. I wander between two shelves I've never explored before.

"Why?" I hear her call. Then, "Where are you?"

"I'm in land grants and sewage plans," I answer, wrinkling my nose as I read the spines of the huge ledgers lining the shelves. "I'm looking for stuff on the historical society."

"You're *in* the historical society," Maude says, appearing next to me.

"Yeah, but who runs it?" I ask. "Is there a record of who have been members?"

"You're wondering if Ms. Lyle was a member?"

"Kind of," I answer. "She seems really interested in our project, like maybe it's something she's personally invested in."

"Why don't you just ask her?"

"I will," I answer. "I just thought I'd check here first."

Maude guides me down and up aisles until we get to a low bookshelf next to the window on the opposite end of the attic from our little nook. "Here are the member rosters," she says. "Ms. Lyle is maybe seventy-five, so here are the ones for the past sixty or so years, on the off chance she joined up when she was eighteen, the youngest age a person can be a member."

I spend the afternoon flipping through but don't see her name anywhere.

"Also," Maude says, later reappearing next to me, "I found something that might interest you."

"Really?" I ask, turning to see the small piece of paper she is holding in her fingers.

"I found it in the repair box. Apparently, it was separated from the book. Shall we tape it back in?"

I have to blink at the page like fifty times before my brain really understands what I'm seeing.

"It's the rest of the poem?" I ask weakly.

Maude grins. "Well, part of it anyway. Someone really ripped this book to shreds. It's a start, though. Come on."

I follow her back to the green metal desk, where she pulls a length of clear tape from a heavy holder and carefully seals the torn page back into the book.

"There's at least a little more to it now," Maude says.

"Oh my gosh," I breathe. I get out my phone first, snapping a picture and texting it to Zooey with about a million exclamation points.

The newly found part of the poem reads:

Alone in this you will be,
Except your guide and the one who sees.

"The one who sees?" I ask aloud, confused. "Your guide? What the heck does that mean?"

Maude shrugs. "Who knows. Poets are weird."

The one who sees. Could Maude actually see what's happening to me? Could she be my guide? I look hard at her. She blinks at me, looking totally confused.

Okay, maybe not.

My mind keeps me awake, whirring all night.

Zooey is out again on Wednesday, and I'm back at my old friends' table. For the very first time. Again. I wish I could figure out if it really was a flash of recognition I saw in Fee's eyes and, if it was, what I did to get it there. The whole *one who sees* thing has me feeling so strange, I'm watching everyone, trying to figure out if someone is watching me.

"Hi!" Piper says, swallowing. "Are you new . . ."

"Yep, I'm new here," I answer quickly. "Hey, did you guys know I'm from Brooklyn?"

I watch Fee's eyes widen, wait for her to ask me about it.

"Oh, it was *incredible*," I say. "I mean, I was, like, living the dream, you know. People come from all over the world to live there, and I was *born* there. It was just awesome." I go into a long story about the subway, and when I finish, Fee looks interested, but there is no flicker of recognition on her face.

I don't even realize Zooey came back to school the next day until I'm about to sit down by Piper.

"Hold it," Zooey says, making a sudden appearance worthy of Maude.

"Hey, you're back!" I say happily. "Did you come in after first period?"

"Yes, I'm back," she says to me. And then to my former friends, whom I was impressing with tales of Brooklyn street art, "I have to borrow her." She leads me to the far end of the cafeteria where the snack machine stands.

I stand facing her, my arms crossed over my long-sleeved kitten sweatshirt. "Are you feeling better?" I ask.

"You have to knock it off," she says firmly.

"Knock *what* off?" I ask, leaning hard against the soda machine, before I realize the front is made of plastic that pushes in when you lean on it. It ends up kind of hugging me. I straighten up, and there is a big clonking sound as the plastic pops back out.

"I had no idea this is what you were up to while I was gone. I thought you were still hanging in the library with Zubki."

I shrug, a little defensively. "There were no more books to be shelved. And you weren't here, so I needed company."

"I think they've made it pretty clear they don't want your company, Hattie," Zooey says, sounding a little bitter.

"They've made it clear?" I ask, freeing myself from the

soda machine. A weird, tingly feeling crawls up the back of my neck.

"That they don't want to be friends with you. I mean, seriously, day after day, I see you talk to them and they're nice to your face, and then they ignore you the next day! And now you're sitting with them? Are you, like, a glutton for punishment or something?!"

"You see them ignore me?" I ask, my brain whirring as I realize what she's saying.

"Yeah, day after day. They don't want to be friends with you, Hattie. Sorry if that's harsh, but I feel like you're just not getting it. Let it go. They defriended you. Get over it."

"So you've seen me talk to them?"

Zooey makes a frustrated noise. "Are you even listening to me? *Everyone* has seen you talking to them. Just no one else wants to tell you how sad it makes you look."

"You've seen me. Talking to them?"

"YES!" she says loudly. "Hattie, they are messing with you. They're never going to be friends with you. Trust me, this used to be, like, my *career.*"

My mouth goes dry, my heart is racing. "Will you do me a favor?"

Her eyes narrow a bit. "Maybe. What?"

"Will you go over there and ask them if they know me?"

"Why . . . why are you *such* a glutton for punishment? Of course they'll say they don't know you! They're freezing you out, Hattie. I should know what that looks like. It's what happened to me."

I nod. "I know. Just, just go over."

"Fine," she says, and I watch as she marches over. Piper and Celeste look up and smile at her. Fee does, too, but her whole body stiffens as she does. I watch as Zooey motions toward me, and my former friends look over to where I stand. They shake their heads; Fee says something. Zooey says something back, something I guess might be a little mean. Because I see Piper look hurt and shake her head again. I watch as Zooey keeps talking, and they keep looking over at me, shaking their heads.

By the time Zooey is walking back toward me, I'm heading out of the cafeteria. She follows me down the hall, calling after me to hold up, but I don't stop, not until I'm in the last stall of the girls' bathroom in the science wing, the one that no one uses because it's so far away.

"Hattie, what is going on?" Zooey asks, leaning against the open stall door of orange-painted metal. "I asked them; they pretended they'd just met you. Jerks."

"They should call this the sherbet bathroom," I say nervously, taking in the gleaming orange and white tiles. "Or maybe the Creamsicle bathroom? Why don't we use this place ever? This bathroom is, like, the best."

"Hattie, what is going—"

"I think you might be"—my heart races with what I'm about to say, and I think I might get dizzy, so I sit down on the toilet, grateful the lid is closed—"I think you might be my *one who sees*."

"Who sees *what?*"

"Alone in this you will be,
Except your guide and the one who sees."

"Are you talking about the Harvest Jinx?" she asks, and she steps away from the stall door, making it swing a little. "The part of the poem you texted me yesterday?"

"Yes," I say, my stomach lurching as I continue. "I am going to tell you the truth. The truth that I've been hiding from you and Maude and everyone else."

"Okay," she says slowly.

I take a deep breath. "I've been jinxed, and I think you're the one who can see it."

I hold my breath, watching as she looks at me, blinking. *Oh please oh please oh please oh please don't forget me.*

"Ugh, Hattie, what are you talking about!" Her voice echoes off the Creamsicle tiles.

I break into a huge smile, jump off the toilet, and hug her.

"*Gah!* No hugging in the bathroom! You were just on the john!" she says, pulling out of my grasp, moving to the sink, and filling her palms with foaming soap from the dispenser.

"You know me! You really know me!" I say weepily, leaning against the sink next to hers and smiling.

"This again?" She cranks the paper-towel dispenser. "Hattie, of course I know you!"

"But my friends don't! I swear to you, Zooey, they don't remember me. They don't remember meeting me, becoming best friends, none of it. And no one else here remembers I was ever friends with them either. Everyone has just sort of . . . forgotten."

"Except me?" she asks incredulously, tossing the paper towels.

"Except you. Because you're—"

"The one who sees. Right. So," she says, stepping around me and toward the bathroom door. "You just stay here. I'm going to go crazy-check your little theory, and I'm going to come back in with your former friends so they can apologize for sending you over the deep end, and I'm going to bring in a couple of other people to tell that they do in fact remember that you were friends with them and that you are now in fact making a fool of yourself on a daily basis trying to get back into their good graces. Stay here. BRB, okay?"

"Okay!" I say breathlessly. "I'll just wait here."

And I do wait there. For a long time. So long that I think maybe Zooey forgot about me, or maybe got in trouble for leaving the cafeteria without a hall pass. I'm about to go look for her, when the bathroom door slowly opens again, and Zooey steps in.

"I was . . ." she says, shaking her head, like she is trying to make sense of something. "I was going to get the guidance counselor and bring her in to you. Because I was kind of worried you had maybe lost touch with reality or something?" She stands in front of the sink, looking at her own reflection. "But then I thought, *Why not just ask someone about what Hattie said?* So I did. And then I asked someone else, because that first someone was from way below the loser line, so what would they know about anything anyway? But then the next person I asked said the same thing: *Hattie was never friends with Piper. Or Celeste. Or Fee.* So I asked someone else. And someone else after that . . ." She trails off, then turns to face me. "Hattie, were you jinxed?"

I nod.

She hugs me this time and says, "This is so weird!"

"I know!" I say gleefully. "It's terrible! And now you get to know about it, too!"

"So what do we do?" she asks, finally pulling away.

"About what?" I ask.

"The jinx, how do we break the jinx?"

I burst out laughing. "Seriously?"

"Yeah, seriously!" she says. "I can't be the only one who knows about this weirdness! I'll go crazy, like you."

"Well, get ready to go bananas, sister, because there is no way to break a Harvest Jinx. You read the poem, you know what it said!"

"Okay, fine. So I'm the one who sees? Who's the guide?"

We look at each other and say at the same time, "Maude."

"Do you think she knows?" Zooey asks. "That she's your . . . guide or whatever? We have to ask her."

"NO!" I say loudly. "We can't."

"What? Why?"

"Because what if we tell her about the jinx and then it gets worse? That rule is no joke. I broke it soon after I was jinxed, and that's the reason my friends keep forgetting me every single new day."

"We have to try," Zooey says.

chapter Twenty-four

I keep expecting Zooey to be the first to speak, and I think she thinks I'm going to say something, so we end up just standing there, breathing in Maude's general direction.

She stares up at us from behind the huge desk for a long time and then says, "Yes?"

Zooey and I exchange a look.

"I've been jinxed," I say.

Maude is quiet for a moment. She swivels in her chair. "Interesting."

"Interesting?" Zooey asks. "Don't you mean *No way, that's not possible, I've spent the last several weeks telling you that the Harvest Jinx doesn't exist?*"

Maude shrugs.

"So you believe us?" I ask, kind of disappointed that Zooey and I don't have to go through the whole explanation we'd practiced on the way over.

"It's unexpected, that's for sure," Maude says. "I don't know of anyone who's actually been jinxed. I really did think it was just a story." She's quiet for a moment as she looks to Zooey. "And you're her seer?"

Zooey nods.

"So I must be your guide!" Maude says, looking pleased. "Interesting! Now, explain. From the beginning."

I'm glad for the chance to tell the story, and Zooey fills in the things I forget. We tell her all about the Friendship Pact, about my friends forgetting me, and then *really* forgetting me.

When we're done Maude looks at me thoughtfully. "So, what did you do?"

"What do you mean, what did I do?" I ask.

"What did you do to break this . . . Friendship Pact."

"That's the thing!" I say. "I didn't do anything! I've been over that day a million times in my head, and I can't think of a single thing I did."

Maude keeps studying me before finally saying, "Okay."

"So"—Zooey directs the question to Maude—"what do we do?"

"Yeah," I say, "you need to, like . . . guide me."

"I don't know that there is anything to do," Maude says, her interest waning. "We just wait out the jinx until the end of the year, and then young Hattie will be free."

"We can do that," Zooey says confidently. "At least you'll be able to talk about it now, right? That'll make it easier."

And we do talk, all of us. I tell them more about moving to Trepan's Grove, about how I was sort of hiding myself. How I was worried that my friends wouldn't like the real me, so I morphed into what I thought they wanted. Zooey talks more, too. It turns out that the whole reason she decided to turn in her mean-girl credentials was because of camp. She was a head camper this year, which is something between a regular camper and a counselor-in-training. She said she'd spent years being a sort of queen of the cabin, basically acting the same way she does at school, just with a different set of girls quaking in her wake. But this year, she had responsibility, and it didn't go well. Not at all. At least at first. Her second week there, she made fun of one of the girls in the cabin she was assigned to, and her head counselor took her aside. Zooey cries as she remembers the story. "She asked me how it made me feel to be so cruel, and asked me how I would feel if a girl I looked up to treated me that way." Zooey sniffed. "I mean, it's stuff I've thought about before. I mean, I'm not a total idiot. I'd just never . . . that little girl was, like, *crushed* that I'd teased her. And I realized that aside from her age, there was nothing different about her and the kids I made fun of at school." So Zooey changed.

She said it wasn't easy; she said it *still* wasn't easy, but by the time she came back to Trepan's Grove, she felt almost like a totally different person. Except nobody noticed. School started, and Zooey didn't say a mean thing about anyone. But she still felt horrible about herself. Because while she didn't say anything mean herself, she just stood there while her friends did. So she told them she didn't want to be like that anymore. And that's when the great defriending happened.

We turn in our project for social studies on the Friday before Christmas break. Everyone in class is sort of giddy, a lot of us passing our projects to one another before we turn them in to Ms. Lyle. I am proud of the work we did; the heavy packet of pages feels good and solid in my hands.

To celebrate, Zooey and I storm the historical society after school, even though Maude tries to stop us at the top of the stairs by declaring, *Visiting hours are Tuesdays and Thursdays from eleven a.m. to five p.m.* She is cracking up laughing before she can even finish her sentence. We gather in our little nook. I have a six-pack of purple Fizzy Fuzz, Zooey brought cheese crackers, and Maude provides long, salty pretzel sticks. It's a weird combination, but somehow it really works.

With only a week left before New Year's, I am feeling almost a little sad about things ending. What will it be like when my friends remember me? Will Zooey come and hang out with us? Will we still come and visit Maude?

Our first Christmas in Trepan's Grove is amazing. I actually let my parents convince me to hold off on reading the last Tilde's Realm until Christmas morning, and I spend a happy few hours lying under the Christmas tree reading until all of my uncles and aunts and cousins all come up from the city. Everyone is crammed into our kitchen and den, the cousins up in my room, laughing our heads off. I text with Zooey that night, wishing her a merry Christmas and making plans to meet up in a couple of days.

The day after Christmas, I go with Dad to the Dentist's House, and that's when I see something really strange out on the snowy common. Actually, at first I see Zooey standing in the snow by the Chin, her breath puffing out in front of her, her hair tucked under what must be a new snow cap she got for Christmas. I tell Dad where I'm going, and then crunch across the street just as she's turning in my direction.

She doesn't look happy to see me, not at all. In fact, she looks so horrified that my first thought is *Snow Bug*, and I kind of freeze for a second, thinking she's going to yell out that it's crawling on my head. But then from the other side of the Chin come none other than Teagan and Tess. I'm too close to turn back without saying anything. Zooey's already seen me, and so have they.

"Oh, *hi, Hattie!*" Tess says in a voice dripping with sweet. "How was your Christmas?"

"Good," I say, walking closer, keeping my eye on Zooey. Maybe she needs backup, maybe they called her here to defriend her all over again. "How was yours?"

"Oh, it was great," Teagan answers, cutting Tess off before she can say anything.

I nod. "What are you up to today?"

Teagan smiles widely. "We're just hanging out. Want to come?"

I try to read Zooey's face, but I can't. "Sure," I say, not wanting to leave her alone with them. "Where are we going?"

"Nowhere," Zooey says firmly. Then she gulps. "You're not going anywhere with us."

"Oh, come on," Tess says, almost teasing, "she wants to come!"

"Well, I don't want her to," Zooey says. She looks at me. "I don't want you to come, okay?"

"Wh . . . wh . . ." I can't even get out the word *why*.

"Because you're a loser, that's why. I've been hanging

out with you as a joke. Just get lost, okay? Go back to your daddy and stay there."

She says this with such venom, with such an angry tremor in her voice, that I don't even respond. I just back away, and then turn and walk quickly back to my dad's office, tears burning and then chilling in my eyes.

She texts me later that night, and I don't respond. I don't respond the next day, either, or the day after that.

chapter
twenty-five

"Hattie." I look up from where I'm patting a snowman's belly into a perfectly round pooch in the little patch of snow-covered lawn in front of our town house. It's New Year's Eve day, and I plan on sticking a sparkler in this guy's snow hand when midnight comes.

The white fake fur on the hood of Zooey's anorak blends in with the low white sky behind her. Snowflakes snag as they fall, making it look like her face is surrounded by a crystal halo. She kicks at the snow with her Nordic boots, her hands shoved deep into her pockets. "I texted you," she says, her breath puffing before it disappears.

I shrug, my snow pants making *zippy zip zip* sounds as I scoot on my knees to the other side of the snowman and start patting. "I saw."

"Why didn't you text me back?" she asks, her boots crunching through the snow as she moves closer to me.

"Why should I?" I ask, breathless from my work. I sit back on my heels, wipe my nose with the wrist part of my mitten.

Her huffy breath expands and dissolves in the cold air. "Because I have something to show you."

I roll my eyes. "You showed me plenty."

"Hattie, won't you let me explain?" she says, annoyed.

"What? You explained just fine. You explained how I'm a loser, and we're not even friends. I guess that's what's going to happen once my jinx breaks, right? What going back to normal means to you? You'll go back to standing around while the Ts eviscerate people? Or I guess you're going to be mean again? Making kids at summer camp cry? I hope the Ts never get on your bad side, because they may be mean, but you"—I shake my head—"you must have coal in your chest instead of a heart."

Zooey reels back a little at this, and even though she hurt me, I'm immediately sorry I did the same to her.

"I'm sorry," I say quickly, stepping forward, but she just shakes her head quickly and pulls a small flat package out of her pocket.

"Ms. Lyle was over for Christmas," Zooey says, and then, in response to my confused look, "She was my mom's teacher, too. We have her over every Christmas. Anyway, she was asking about our project, and she said she was disappointed we didn't include anything about the Harvest Jinx. She gave me this, and asked me to give it to you."

She holds the package out to me, but it slips from her mittened hand. I bend down to get it and she says, "Just stop!" She picks it up and shoves it against me, and before I can even see what it is, she's hurrying across the snowy lawn away from me.

I kick as much snow as I can off my boots against the doorframe before I stomp into our foyer, dropping my mittens, flinging off my hat, and wiggling out of my coat and snow pants. It's chilly in the foyer, and as I run upstairs with the package held against me, my skin stings when the warm air hits my cheeks.

"Hot cocoa?" my mom calls as I run past the kitchen and up the stairs.

"Later! Thanks!" I call back. In my room, I scoot under the heavy comforter on my bed, displacing Champ in the process. I'm still so chilly that I pull the blanket over my head, leaving just a little opening so I can see as I open the paper bag. It's a book, an exact copy of the green one from the historical society, the one with half of the Harvest Jinx poem torn out.

I turn to page forty-three.

"Oh, CRAP!" I yell, jumping out of bed and running downstairs, holding tight to the book. Nothing I was wearing has had a chance to dry, and since I didn't hang it up, everything has freezing-cold wet spots, but I pull on my snow pants, coat, mittens, and hat anyway and rush out the door. "GOING TO ZOOEY'S! I HAVE MY PHONE!" I yell up the stairs on my way out, just as I hear the teakettle whistle with boiling water for my hot chocolate.

Running in the snow is no easy task, and I totally understand the appeal of sled dogs. Zooey's just turned the corner of our street when I see her, and I'm guessing the sound of me huffing and puffing and gasping for air is enough for her to turn around and mercifully wait for me to catch up.

"You saw it?" she asks, raising her chin.

I nod, holding up a finger for her to wait until I catch my breath. Of course, because I'm wearing mittens, it looks like I'm holding up my whole hand. She high-fives me.

"What . . . what . . . what are we going to do?" I ask.

"We need to find Maude," she answers.

The little ceramic Christmas tree sitting on Maude's big green desk at the historical society gives a festive glow to page forty-three as Maude bends over it, reading it for the third time.

"This is not good," Maude says finally, looking up at us.

"We know!" we answer in unison.

She turns the book to the side, so we can all once again read the full text of the poem:

> Every year at Harvesttime is the moment to
> remind
> That what you say and what you mean should
> have nothing in between.
> All twenty-four hours of Festival day,
> Be aware of what you say,
> For make a promise before you think,
> And you could get a Harvest Jinx!
> A jinx will last 'til the New Year dawns
> One minute past midnight, and it will be gone.
> Alone in this you will be,
> Except your guide and the one who sees.
> Tell no one else your tale of woe
> Or you will see how wrong things can go.
> It is up to you to find the ones
> You have wronged with the things you've
> done.
> Tell them the truth you sought to hide
> With a promise that was a lie.
> Tell the truth and be set free
> Or you will stay jinxed for eternity.

"Eternity," Zooey says quietly. "And I thought 'til New Year's Eve was harsh."

I look at her and Maude. "What am I going to do? It's New Year's Eve." I look at the clock. "Midnight is just a few hours away!"

"It's obvious!" Zooey says impatiently. "You have to find the ones you've wronged! You have to make it right or you'll be jinxed forever!"

"But I didn't do anything wrong!" I object. "The Friendship Pact was about lying and gossiping, and I didn't do either of those things." I'm in tears now, feeling truly hopeless.

Zooey blinks at me. "Really?"

"What do you mean?" I ask, gulping.

"I mean you've kind of been lying since you moved here."

"I have not!"

"She's right," Maude says, giving Zooey an impressed nod. "You weren't honest with your friends about what you like."

"You think I got jinxed because I didn't tell them I'm a nerd?!" I yelp. Then I get quiet. Then I whisper, "Holy crow. I bet you're right."

chapter twenty-six

"Chez Packenbush is packed," Maude says as we make our way up the walk to Piper's front steps. When we get to the top step, I pause before reaching for the doorbell.

I turn to Maude and Zooey. "What if it doesn't work?"

"It'll work," they say in unison. Zooey reaches around me and rings the doorbell.

"I want you to know," I say, "that if I, like, somehow forget everything that's happened, I just want you guys to know how much I love that you helped me."

"You're not going to, like, disappear or something," Zooey says.

"You don't know that!" I say. "What if I do this wrong and I vanish and there's just a steaming baked potato or something in my place?"

Maude wrinkles her nose. "Starchy."

From inside Piper's house, there is an argument going on about who will answer the door, and the sounds of some sort of struggle. Finally, the door creaks open half an inch before being slammed shut and Piper's voice is saying, "Peanut! You can't open the door without a grown-up or at least me."

The door opens again. Piper and Peanut are both in pajamas, wearing sparkly glasses in the shape of next year's number. Beyond them, I see Fee and Celeste sitting at the kitchen island.

"Hi!" Piper says. She looks beyond me at Zooey and Maude. "Oh, hey, Zooey. And Maude! Oh my gosh!" She hollers over her shoulder, "PAOLA, Maude Faem's here!"

"She has something to tell you," Zooey says to Piper, nudging me.

"Oh, cool, are you like selling something? Come in!"

We follow her into the kitchen.

"I want to tell you who I—"

"Do you want hot chocolate?"

"Oh, sure . . ."

"Okay, wait, you were saying?"

"I want to tell you who I—"

"Marshmallows?"

"Sure. I want to tell you who I—"

"I didn't have to work at the farm stand yesterday!" Fee bursts out, her voice loud and thick with emotion.

"What?" Celeste and Piper say at the same time.

Fee's mouth wavers. "I was at Teagan's house!"

"Why?" Celeste asks.

"The 'After-Christmas Gift Swap'?" Zooey asks ruefully.

Fee nods, her face now streaming with tears.

"What the heck is an after-Christmas gift swap?" Piper asks.

"It's . . . it's . . ." Fee can't get out the sentence.

Zooey clears her throat. "It's when Teagan and Tess"—she pauses—"and me. At least it used to be . . . It's when they invite you over with your favorite Christmas presents and trick you into trading them for something crappy."

"That is awful!" Celeste says, and I can tell she's angry at Fee for lying about where she'd been, but she pulls her into a hug anyway.

"That's really a thing?" Piper says in shock. "Like they . . . YOU . . . actually do that? I've never even heard of it!" She grabs a Santa Claus dish towel off the counter and hands it to Fee, who blows her nose.

"I don't. Not anymore," says Zooey. "And the reason you never heard of it is because we usually would choose someone who was Upper Popular, someone who thought they had an actual chance of getting with us. We'd swear them to secrecy."

"After you stole their stuff?" I ask angrily, looking hard

at Zooey. How could she have been a part of something like that?

"Yes," she answered. "They . . . we thought it was a funny joke."

"Some joke," Celeste says. "I can't believe you ever hung out with them."

Fee nods and gulps. "That's why they invited me. They said now that Zooey is out of the picture, they need a third person."

Zooey's face clouds at this, and I wonder if she really did still hope they would take her back. But then she says, "I knew they were messing with Fee. I tried to stop them." She turns to me, a person I realize they don't even know. "That's what I was doing that day out on the common, when I told you to go away."

Fee continues her story. "They said I can sit with them at lunch when school starts again. But I don't even want to sit with them! I want to sit with you guys!"

"Good," Zooey says, "because they'll text you the morning of the first day of school and say they take it back."

"You were going to ditch us?" Celeste asks quietly.

Piper's eyes widen. "Seriously, Fee, you don't want to be friends with us anymore?"

"Of course I do!" Fee wails. "I just . . . I just wanted to see what it was like. You know"—she twists the Santa towel miserably—"to have the popular kids like me."

"Wait a minute!" Celeste practically yells, staring at Fee, who immediately looks down at the twisted towel in her hands. "You have been acting weird for weeks. Is that what this is all about? Have you been, like, trying out for them?"

Zooey's face changes, like a dawn of recognition. "That's why you chopped your bangs."

Fee nods. "They said I had to."

Piper gasps. "And why you've barely been eating at lunch!"

"They said I was fat."

Celeste looks so angry she might pop. "I would never say that to you," she growls quietly.

"I know," Fee says.

"You're not fat!" Piper says.

"I know," Fee says again.

"Then why would you go along with it?" Celeste asks.

"Because they said it was the one thing keeping me out of their group," Fee says, starting to cry again. "I'm just embarrassed."

"Fee, you're not—"

"I KNOW I'm not fat!" she says loudly, angrily. "But I don't have the same body you guys do, and I *know* that's fine, I know I'm strong and that I'm healthy and I'm pretty. I just . . . I'm just embarrassed I let them make me forget."

Celeste and Piper are quiet at this, and I'm so caught up

in the drama that it takes a nudge from Zooey to remind me of why I'm here.

"My name is Hattie. I'm twelve. And I . . . I like T-shirts with cats on them. And I like this book series called Tilde's Realm. And I hate field hockey. I mean, like, I really hate it. It's just an awful game."

Zooey mouths the words *Move on*.

"Um. Okay, also. I like—"

I'm interrupted by loud voices from the living room, where Peanut and her mom are shouting, "TEN! NINE!"

I look in terror at Zooey.

"Keep going!" she says.

"And, um, even though I like happy songs, really I like sad songs better and, um, I hate the way corduroys make a zippy sound when I walk . . ." Why isn't anything changing? I've said everything I was supposed to say! So I just keep babbling. "And, um, I wear my socks inside out because I don't like the way the seams feel, and when I'm in the shower, I catch water in my mouth and then spit it out like I'm a fountain and . . ." Zooey looks pretty much horrified at this point.

"FOUR! THREE!"

I remember something.

"TWO!"

"I! HATE! APPLE! PIE!"

"HAPPY NEW YEAR!"

There is instant noise and color, then happy shouts from outside on the common, from the television, from everyone in the crowded kitchen. Squeals as Peanut runs into the kitchen, scrambles up onto the island, and throws handfuls of confetti. Somebody—or many somebodies—bangs on pots and pans with wooden spoons; music starts, and there's jumping and dancing, kids, adults, everyone.

Zooey looks questioningly at me through the people and the showers of confetti flying through the air. *Did it work?* her face asks. I shrug. *I don't know!*

Then Piper is right in front of me, a huge smile on her face. "I've been holding on to this for months!" she shouts above the din. She pushes a small, silver-wrapped present into my hands. I tug the present open, and I find the gyrgone I admired at the Harvest Festival, before everything went bananas. Piper jumps up and down. "I went back and bought it because I could TELL you wanted it! Do you like it?" she asks.

"I LOVE IT!" I practically scream, and then she has my wrists, and she's pulling me and laughing, swinging me in a circle, around and around and around. The colors blur; the sounds do, too; my heart lifts in joy. As we turn, Fee and Celeste bounce around us, doing their ice-skating routine and cracking up. Through the blur, I see Zooey across the kitchen, standing next to Maude, wry grins on their faces. I close my eyes and enjoy the spin.

EPILOGUE

"**H**attie Hattie Hattie Cakes!" the voices call. I jump up from the rocking chair on the front porch of the Dentist's House and wave when I see Piper, Celeste, and Fee looking up and grinning at me from the flower-lined sidewalk.

"Hold on!" I say, then call in through the open window to ask Lucia to please tell my dad I'm going across the street.

"Okay!" I say, linking arms with Piper as we head across the street onto the common. "Are you *sure* there's nothing I need to know about the Apple Blossom Festival?"

Celeste smirks at Fee and then grins back at me. "Hattie's still convinced she was jinxed at Harvest Festival."

"I was!" I practically croon in mock offense. I know there is no way they will believe me. It seems that's how the jinx was set up: As soon as things are back to normal, it's as if the jinx never happened. That photo-booth strip from the Harvest Festival? As soon as the jinx broke, my friends reappeared in the pictures. Those many weeks I spent hanging out with Zooey, and with Maude, researching in the historical society, seem to my friends like they lasted only as long as a hiccup. They are entirely unconcerned with the weeks-long gap in our collective memory, as if it doesn't matter at all. And really, I guess, it doesn't matter to them. All they know is that we're friends, same as we have been since I moved here. And I guess that's all that really matters to me, too.

As for Zooey, well, I wouldn't say we're friends, more like . . . warm acquaintances. After New Year's, she started hanging out with the Upper Popular kids, just like everyone expected her to do in the first place. And even though the Upper Popular kids aren't totally evil, they still don't hang out with us Lower Medium Popular kids. Especially since one of us is a one hundred percent nerd. That's right, ever since the whole jinx fiasco, I've made it my mission to be myself one hundred percent of the time. No more zippy corduroys. No more sports played on fields. Fee and Celeste keep trying to get me and Piper to go skating with them—that's right, Fee is Back on the Ice!—but we prefer to just cheer their competitions from the stands. While drinking hot cocoa. And now my life involves lots and lots of sci-fi and fantasy read out in the open where everyone can see. And what's amazing, and what I could have predicted if I'd just stopped worrying so much, is that my friends totally don't care. They like me, cat T-shirts and all.

Of course, not everyone is a fan. Teagan and Tess are still total mean girls, and they're still trying to find someone to be the third point on their triangle of doom. But after what they put Fee through last winter got out, nobody's biting. They'll mutter mean comments at us sometimes when we walk by, but at this point it's pretty easy to just ignore them.

Maude went back to teach at MIT without telling me and Zooey. We only found out she'd left because we went to thank her for her help when we got our paper back from Ms. Lyle. We got an A+, thank you very much. But it wasn't Maude behind the big green metal desk, it was her mom. "She left something for you," her mom said when we introduced ourselves. And when she stepped behind a bookshelf to get it, I was kind of hoping it was a letter or a card or maybe a painting. Something from the heart, you know? But when Maude's mom stepped back out, Zooey and I both cracked up. She was holding a six-pack of Fizzy Fuzz.

"So, what time is she getting here?" Piper asks, as we step onto the common.

"In about an hour," I say, suddenly nervous. Apparently, I'm not the only one.

"Do you think she'll like us?" Fee asks. "I mean, she's from Brooklyn. That's, like, a whole other kind of cool."

"*I'm* from Brooklyn," I remind her.

"Yeah, but you're *Hattie*. That's different," Fee insists.

"What if we don't like her?" Celeste asks.

"You don't have to like her," I answer. One thing I realized about Celeste: She doesn't like being told who she has to like. That's why she was sometimes prickly to me. She never got the chance to decide she wanted to be my friend. She just got home from skating camp and I was plopped in her lap, just like her little half brother.

"Well, you have pretty good taste in friends so far," Celeste says wryly. "So I bet she's okay."

My heart does a little flutter. All of my friends, together in one place. It strikes me that this might not have been possible without the jinx. If I had kept trying to be someone I'm not, I'm not sure my friendships with Piper and Fee and Celeste and Rae could have lasted. And I definitely would never have met Maude, or become friends with Zooey. I do know one thing for sure: My friends like me for who I am, and I don't need any sort of pact to prove it.

Acknowledgments

This book would not be possible without the love, patience, and encouragement of my mom and dad and big brother; my husband, Jeff Salane; my agent, Tracey Adams; and my editor, Lisa Ann Sandell. I cannot tell you how grateful I am to all of you for your support. It has meant the world to me. And to David Levithan, who said, "I think you have a middle grade novel in you," and gave me the chance to see he was right. And to Champion Coffee: You have given me a wonderful place to work on every book I have ever written, so I named a cat after you.

About the Author

Adrienne Maria Vrettos lives with her family in Brooklyn, New York, where she writes middle grade and young adult fiction. Find her online at AdrienneMariaVrettos.com.

31901060402536